THE DARKNESS OF LIGHT:

THE CRYSTAL OF LIGHT

a novel by
Hap Lea

The Darkness of Light:
The Crystal of Light
by Hap Lea
Copyright © 2011 by Hurdle H. Lea IV

Hurdle H. "Hap" Lea IV
5 East 22nd Street, Suite 28-M
New York, New York 10010
212-598-1044 or hap@hap-lea.com

ISBN: 0615474950
ISBN-13: 9780615474953

The publisher shares the opinion that creative fiction is an art form and believes that the author, as an artist, should have the right to present the art in its original form and to make changes in their manuscripts, including feedback from readers themselves, at which point a new edition will be published.

Hap Lea: hap@hap-lea.com
Website: www.hap-lea.com

For my grandparents,
GrandDiddle, GranChic,
Turtle, and Paw-Paw.

Table of Contents

Prologue 1

Chapter 1 - 10 Years Later, the Warning..............9

Chapter 2 - The Story Begins 13

Chapter 3 - Confrontation on the Train...........21

Chapter 4 - Finding Zan 29

Chapter 5 - Back at the Academy......................41

Chapter 6 - The Fragment, the Dream.............59

Chapter 7 - Leaving Friends 69

Chapter 8 - The Legend of the Crystal of
        Light...89

Chapter 9 - Race to the Coast...........................101

Chapter 10 - Fragments in the Sand 111

Chapter 11 - Memories that won't be
        Forgotten 117

Chapter 12 - Jeremy's Hideout........................131

Chapter 13 - The Battle where it all began......137

Chapter 14 - Learning a New Way of Spell
        Casting..143

Chapter 15 - It has only just begun 159

Chapter 16 - Winter Party and Crow's
                    Warning..169
Epilogue 173
Acknowledgments.............................175
About the Author................................179

Prologue

The night was quiet, the houses had all gone dark; a gust of wind shook the trees and made the grass dance. Far from the village, the Temple of the Monks lay high on the hill. Past the gates to the temple, through the entrance door and inside, the halls were filled with paintings and artifacts of the Holy. At the end of the long corridor, the forbidden steps lead down to a door painted black. Inside, hidden from the world, was a crystal unlike any other. It had a story to tell. The monks had placed the crystal there, hidden from the world and sealed inside a glass urn for a very good reason. And there it stayed until that fateful night when that which they feared more than anything would come true.

Footsteps echoed quietly down the steps, the door gently opened and a hooded man peeked inside; the light that the crystal emitted stuns him. The light gave the room an eerie feeling. He closed the door behind him and walked towards the urn.

"At last!" he said as he carefully lifted the glass urn and removed the crystal, holding it up for a better look. This was the treasure for which he had come.

"With this now in our possession, we will show those accursed White Witches and the rest of the world what fear really is." The light faded as the hooded man hid the crystal in the pocket of his cloak.

He retraced his steps in near darkness and reopened the door, stepped out and closed the door silently behind him. Back in the hallway, he made his way back outside. He never noticed the silent monk in prayer, however the monk noticed him as he rushed down the corridor, for they had known that eventually someone would come. The monk rushed to alert the others that there was an intruder and they hurried to pursue the man. Outside the temple, the monks caught sight of the intruder and ordered him to stop; the man lowered his hood and turned to the monks, not frightened in the least.

"I think we all know what my answers going to be," he said as he smiled. "So allow me to show you who you're dealing with."

He then raised his left hand and a thin red line of light shot at the monks; they quickly fled from where they were standing and took cover behind anything they could find. The man then took aim at one of the monks hiding behind a flowerpot and the monk cowered, narrowly escaping sure death!

"Alright, that's enough!" shouted a voice from the temple entrance. The man smiled again taking interest in his new problem.

"Ah, Henry, I was wondering when you would show up." Both men took out ancient, ragged books from the pockets of their cloaks.

"Dean!" Henry shouted, "You shouldn't have come here!" Dean raised his free hand and his book glowed with red light.

"Oh save it, the monks knew that this would happen as did you and your clan." Henry then raised his free hand also, holding his book in the other. But instead of the red light that earlier shot from Dean's fingertips, this was a pale yet iridescent light blue. Both men then began to attack each other, shooting bursts of light from their fingertips. The monks watched in amazement. Neither man allowed the other to catch him off guard; they both knew what was at stake here. Even as the monks hid from the fight, they could not help but watch, they too knew that whatever happened here would affect the world.

"You've got to hand it to these spell casters," whispered one of the monks, hiding with another behind the steps of the temple entrance.

"They are good at that for which they are known and we must pray that Henry is victorious."

After what seemed like hours of combat, the two spell casters were nearing exhaustion. With one last lunge, Henry reached for the spot in Dean's cloak where the crystal was hidden. Just as he touched his target, Dean's left hand held a green flame with which he hit Henry in the stomach. Henry dropped his spell book, falling to his knees next to the well-worn book.

"Now what was the point in doing that?" Dean asked, laughing as he looked down at Henry, whose hand was still clutching on to the cloak.

"Whatever it was, it was pointless. It just cost you your life." Dean made a move with his right hand to remove Henry's grip on his cloak, when he did Henry reached out his right arm and grabbed Dean's arm. Now it was Henry's turn to smile.

"Actually, there's a very good reason why I did that," he said as he looked up at Dean. Henry's spell book began to glow again and both of his hands now had purple flames. With his last breath he said "Despirum." Dean dropped his spell book as the monks peeked out of their hiding spots, stunned at the sight of both Masters as they became engulfed in green flames. The crystal which was now floating above the two men started to spin faster and faster and the glow turned the flames blue. Henry fell face first to the ground as the flames died. Dean looked down as his hands as they started to turn to dust and went down onto his knees.

"Y...you." he said still in shock. "What did you do to me? I am sorry, I have failed my master." Then he looked down to where the other man had fallen. "Henry, well played my old friend, but you know we will never give up! My clan is not weak, unlike yours." He then vanished into dust and out of nowhere the wind began to howl and it carried Dean's ashy remains up into the night, all that was left of the intruder were his black cloak, jeans, and brown shoes. The crystal continued to spin around and around then suddenly and without warning, shot up in the night sky and began to crack; it then burst into hundreds of pieces and the fragments shot in every direction through the dark sky. They were scattered across the land and beyond. It was like watching hundreds of shooting stars, soaring through the night sky.

"The power of that spell must've done that," said one of the monks apprehensively, now coming out of his hiding spot. He rushed toward Henry; the rest of the monks followed and they all froze for a moment looking up at the sparks in the sky.

"So now it begins, doesn't it?" asked another monk, "The two clans will start to find and collect the fragments of the crystal."

"Yes," said the monk who now crouched at Henry's side. He looked at the other monks in despair as he felt for a pulse.

"He's dead." He then told another monk to get a message to the White Witches as soon as possible and let them know what had happened. He knew that he must be the one to take the terrible news to Henry's wife. He also knew she would not be surprised that her husband had died a hero, rescuing the crystal from the hands of an enemy. He then looked up once again at the night sky and with a heavy sigh said. "The White Witches must find and collect all the fragments before the Akolt do, for if evil rebuilds the crystal back to its original form before the White Witches do." He closed Henry's eyes with the tips of his fingers; "The results will bring out the worst for us and for the world."

CHAPTER 1

☙❧

10 Years Later, the Warning

It was a very dark night, windy and icy cold. No one would be out in this weather unless they had to be which pleased the people at this meeting, for none of them wished to be seen. The secluded house on the lake had its lights dimmed and there were people talking inside. Light from the fireplace flickered through the windows onto the shrubs surrounding the house. Outside there were two guards keeping watch, one on each side of the door. They both wore long, black cloaks and jeans; the only difference in their clothing was their shoes.

One of them looked at the other and whispered, "What do you think they're talking about in there?" she asked curiously.

"I don't know, but whatever it is, it must be really important since we were told to stay out here and keep watch; Michael will let us know if he needs our help," said the other.

Inside the house, a cloaked man was pacing. Two men also wearing hooded cloaks flanked a man sitting in a chair next to the fireplace.

As the fire roared, the man in the chair said, "I do hope you know what this means, Michael." Looking at Michael who was still pacing, the hooded man in the chair took a deep breath and sat forward. He wore the same black cloak and jeans as Michael and the two guards standing outside with the only difference being that he and the two men standing on each side of him had a symbol on their cloaks; the symbol was the letter A, embroidered in bright red. This single difference highlighted how very different the groups were. The three of them had come to deliver a message.

"We believe the White Witches have gone their separate ways and will no longer be of any threat to us," he said with a grin, very much aware of the type of reaction that was to be expected. Michael stopped pacing and turned; his hazel eyes looked into the eyes of the man in the chair, "Oh yes, they will be a threat, there are still many who haven't yet given up and never will! Especially the children of the men and women your clan members killed ten years ago," he said with confidence. He was clearly standing up for the White Witches and letting the three men know there would be no backing down.

Michael continued. "Marco, I'm afraid you and your master have underestimated us once again. We are as strong and united as ever and our numbers are growing." Marco stood up abruptly, it was now clear to him that Michael and the White Witches would never back down.

"I'm warning you!" Marco said in a threatening voice. "If you or any of the training students at the school get in our way, none of you will ever be safe." He began to laugh at the idea that the White Witches actually believed they had a chance.

"We Akolt like to prolong our enemies suffering as you well know and that is what we intend to do to anyone who stands in our way. This message, I trust, you will pass along to the rest of your clan."

11

The meeting was done without another word; Michael turned and stepped outside quickly into the starless, frigid night and began the trek home with his two follower's right behind him. They disappeared silently into the night.

CHAPTER 2

❧

The Story Begins

Ten years ago something terrible had happened, when a community of people moved to an uninhabited area in Northern Oregon - uninhabited that is but for a very special school. The school was part of the reason why these people chose to move to this area; in fact many of these people had attended the school themselves. The weather was brutal almost year round, but it suited the group just fine. The children were expected to live at the school. Some of the children in this new community were born just like you and me, but others were born with extraordinary abilities. When the Academy opened several decades earlier, the faculty decided that all normal children were prohibited from trying any of the things the gifted children were doing. The faculty knew that if the normal children tried any spells they wouldn't be able to handle the power and they could hurt themselves or the other students. The normal children knew that the gifted students were special, some of them were even brothers or sisters, and all were otherwise treated equally.

One of the extraordinary children was a boy named Kyle Fang; he was a healthy boy of average height from a mortal mother and magic father. He had inherited his mother's light colored eyes and his father's dark hair. The Academy had a name for individuals like him; they were known as half-breeds but it carried no overt stigma. Kyle was considered more impatient than the other children of his kind. When he first arrived at the school, all the other children in his first year class took their time in learning spells, but Kyle always did things his own way. To everyone's surprise, even the teachers knew he had a gift that was far superior to the other children though Kyle often acted before thinking but it was fortunate, for him anyway, that he managed to control his powers. Kyle met Dan, the boy that would become his best friend, the first day Dan moved to the area with his mother at the age of nine.

In Dan's first year of school, Kyle thought he was just another normal kid, but when he came into his class, he then knew that Dan had the same abilities as the other gifted students. The two had their own rivalries, which would continue into adulthood. They were always striving to see who was best and to outdo one another. As the years went by, they became more like brothers. Dan was the one in the class who mostly hid his feelings and rarely took interest in offensive spells. His dark colored eyes and his somewhat long blond hair gave him a sagacious look. Only the school staff knew what happened to his father and they didn't talk about it, but even the students could tell there was sadness in Dan that he kept hidden away from them. During their fourth year at the Academy a girl named May came to the school. Shortly after that her father was hired to teach and moved to a cottage near the boy's dorm. May was put in the same class with Kyle and Dan. She was the type of student who cared for others and did her best in spells of every kind taught at the Academy. Her long brown hair and especially her light blue eyes were inviting, offering a first impression of someone they would like to know. May grew to know both Kyle and Dan very well, and in their fifth year together she began to like Dan a lot. Dan didn't seem to notice, but other students and teachers in the Academy were certain that he did and was too shy to admit it. In the following year the faculty decided to put the fifth year spell-casters into groups with members of the White Witches. Kyle, Dan, and May were placed with a man named Michael and they were thrilled because there wasn't a student at the school who hadn't heard about his abilities. The spell caster students called their group leaders Master.

From that moment on, the spell caster students were assigned missions with their Masters. Michael knew as soon as he met the three students in his group that they were a gifted bunch and would be a group to be reckoned with.

It was now the fifth year at the Academy, but none of the students were prepared for what was to come.

A young teenage boy wearing a black shirt with a brown corduroy jacket and blue jeans was sitting on the windowsill looking outside his dorm room window. He watched as the first year students outside on the lawns read their spell books, pointed their hands at nearby objects, and shouted out the words they just read to themselves. One girl pointed her hand at the ground and shouted "Imolvy!" Flowers grew all around her. Another student was pointing his hand at a tree and shouted. "Morphus!" The tree shook and the leaves turned bight red and orange. All the first year students were casting minor spells enjoying themselves, impressed with their abilities.

"Hey Kyle, hurry up, the Mistress needs to speak with us!" Kyle turned from the window towards the door.

"Alright Dan I'll be right out!" Kyle looked at his spell book for one brief moment in wonder, and then went into the hall where Dan was waiting for him. They both raced down the stairs and then outside. The Mistress' office was on a different side of the school, so they hurried across the big lawn that divided the campus. When they got to the entrance of the main building a teenage girl was waiting inside for them.

"Hi May," said Dan. "Sorry we're late; we should head straight inside the office now before the Headmistress turns us all into door stops." May looked around as they were heading towards the office door. She was watching the normal students working in their classrooms. Sometimes she and the two boys walking with her wondered what

17

their lives would have been if they too had born mortal. Kyle reached his hand out to grab the doorknob as they approached the office.

"Hold on!" said May "We should probably wait for Master Michael."

Kyle lowered his arm. "Some Master," he said, "He's always late."

A voice from inside called out to them "Come in, please." The door opened before Kyle had a chance to open it himself. The Mistress was sitting at a long table with four other adults in the office known as the Assembly Room. She sat in the center with two people on each side of her and they were all facing the door where the children were standing. The panel of adults stared at the young people for a moment and then started to whisper to each other. They abruptly stopped talking as the Mistress stood up. Her long white hair touched the middle of her back as her light green eyes focused on the three kids before her.

"Alright," she said, "Michael isn't here because he's been assigned to go to an important meeting." May raised her hand. "Yes, May what is it?"

"Does this have to do with the Akolt?" she asked. The group of adults at the table nervously glanced at one another.

"Never you mind," said one the men at the table. The Mistress continued, describing what Kyle and his two friends were going to be assigned. As she went on, Kyle couldn't help but wonder why the teachers refused to talk about the Akolt and what type of meeting could be so important that Michael would go alone and not take the three of them with him. He knew that it must have something to do with the Akolt but he also knew that they would not tell him even if that were the case. The teachers just simply ignored questions the students had about this group and they would change the subject whenever the name was mentioned. The only thing the students knew for certain about the clan was that they were called the Akolt and their entire history was forbidden knowledge to any of students.

"Kyle!" said May; she was now looking at him "Did you hear all of that?"

"What?" Kyle looked at May and then at the group at the table.

"Did you hear all the Mistress had to say?"

"Yes, I didn't miss a single word of it." said Kyle. May looked at him disbelievingly as he said, "I heard it! Don't worry about it."

Dan had his eyes closed and his arms crossed, "Oh, please, we both know that he wasn't paying attention while the Mistress was talking."

The Mistress told the three students that since Michael wasn't there, they would have to do this assignment on their own and that the task should be simple. Tomorrow at 6:00 a.m. they would catch the train heading towards a town called Requiem. She handed them each round-trip tickets for the trip.

CHAPTER 3

✿

Confrontation on the Train

The next morning Kyle, Dan and May got up before dawn, dressed quickly, packed their spell books inside their coats and left for the long walk to catch the train. May told Kyle and Dan that the train ride would take the whole day since the town of Requiem was so far away from their village. The gravel path towards the train station was long and winding and the trees along the way were large and almost covered the path, creating a leafy canopy. When the wind blew and the trees moved, shadows were created and they moved back and forth which gave the walk an eerie feeling, almost as if they were being watched. For reasons no one was comfortable voicing, the walk this morning made all three students feel very uneasy. The feeling of uneasiness encouraged them to move even more quickly, or course, and they asked themselves why the school was put so far into the woods away from everything? This was a question they had asked many times but never got a clear answer from anyone. When they arrived at the train station, the train was already waiting and the doors were just opening.

As they climbed the steps onto the train, the conductor said plainly, "Tickets please."

May handed him her ticket and the boys did the same as they followed her into their car. The car was divided into eight separate rooms for comfort and privacy. May was seated with a family of three in Row 31 and as soon as she entered the compartment, she sat down, took out a book and began to read. Dan and Kyle moved farther up and entered their room and flopped down into the comfy train seats. They shared a compartment in Row 28 with an older couple who were talking about the old days and the current gossip.

The old man said, "I hear that there has been a mysterious group of people spotted in the mountains lately."

"I've heard that too," his wife responded. "Do you think it is true that the people in the town of Requiem are concerned?" The husband shook his head.

"Nah. That's just the media exaggerating stories again. Back when I was that young the stories made more sense. And anyway, who the heck would be sneaking around in the mountains and why would anyone, for Pete's sake?"

Back in Row 31, May laid down her book and asked if she could look at the newspaper the father had just finished reading. What caught her attention was the headline and as the man passed her the paper she began to read the caption of the coverphoto.

"The photo above was provided by an eyewitness from the town of Requiem." The photo, although obviously taken from quiet a distance, showed a large group of people gathered around a campfire. The caption continued.

"Eyewitnesses believe they are only travelers camping in the woods and probably not a threat. See page 2 for more of the story."

May turned the page and the article continued, "No one seems to know who this group is. When the police were sent to investigate, the group seemed to have vanished into thin air. Anyone with information on these people should contact the police immediately."

May had a very strange feeling that whatever was happening in the mountains was surely connected to their mission in Requiem and to the Akolt. May went back to her book and the boys did some studying so they wouldn't fall behind in school since they were missing a day of classes. And so the train ride dragged on.

Late in the afternoon as the train was passing through one of the many long granite tunnels on the route to Requiem, it came to a sudden stop. This was very unusual, for the trains were not known to ever stop between towns. There was total silence except the autumn wind howling outside the tunnel's exits. Everyone seemed to be waiting for the conductor to announce the reason for the delay. Then there was total blackness, all of the train lights went out and the passengers sat in darkness. People began to dig flashlights out of their bags and discuss the possible reasons for the stop and loss of lights on the train. The train conductors began to pass from car to car trying to calm the passengers, who by now were in a near state of panic.

"No need to worry!" shouted one of the train's conductors reassuringly, "Just a minor difficulty with the train I am sure, we should be heading on any moment now so just sit back in your seats and we will take care of the problem."

As everyone did what they were told, a little girl began to scream uncontrollably. Her parents tried to calm her down but she couldn't stop crying and could not take her eyes away from the window.

"I saw something out there," she sobbed in a terrified voice. "It was horrible."

No one said anything, but everyone looked at the windows in their rows to reassure themselves there was nothing out there. All they saw was complete darkness. The little girl took her flashlight out of her carry on bag and shined it at the window while her mother continued to calm her and tell her that it was just a bad dream. Suddenly the beam from her the flashlight fell upon something that looked like a hand. The girl moved her light across the window, slightly to the right and the beam hit what appeared to be a man's chest.

"Someone's out there!" shrieked the little girl as the flashlight illuminated the entire body of someone or something. Whatever it was, it began to walk past the windows and headed toward the train door. As it climbed the steps and reached for the door, the train passengers held their breath and sat in total silence. The porter reached for the door to hold it shut but the figure pushed him aside as he entered effortlessly. As the figure entered, the passengers could see from the dim light of their flashlights that whatever had entered was much taller than the conductor. Everyone, including the train's employees, stared in silence. The figure was dressed all in black with a hood, gloves and silken mask that hid its face.

"What were you doing out there?" asked the porter that had been nearly knocked off his feet by the sudden entrance. There was no response to his question and he began to push the train door closed. Just as the door was about to close another black gloved hand stopped the door and again nearly knocked the porter to the ground. A second figure stepped inside the train without saying a word just as the first had. The two split up, moving in opposite directions on the train. The shorter of the two headed towards the back of the train and the taller one took the front. The porter closed the door and looked from one of the figures to the other, as they passed each sleeper car on both left and right they peeked inside and moved on. When the shorter of the two reached Kyle and Dan's car, he stopped completely and ignored the old couple and pointed at Kyle and Dan. Even if the figure didn't speak, the question to Kyle was obvious: "What are you doing on the train?"

"We're only tourists going to explore the town of Requiem," Kyle answered and the figure turned toward Dan and pointed.

"What he said," replied Dan.

The figure stood for a moment and then moved on and explored the remainder of the back of the train. At the same time, the tall one reached May's sleeping car. It stopped and, just like the other, pointed only at May, completely ignoring the other passengers in her car.

"I'm traveling with two friends who are seated farther back, your partner I believe checked them out, we're just exploring some of the nearby towns."

Just as his partner in the back, he too continued to check the train. When the masked figures had searched the entire train they opened the door they had entered through and stepped back outside. The porter at the door stood aside and watched as they disappeared in the darkness. As the door closed behind them, the lights came back on as if nothing had happened and the train began to move on again. Everyone on the train was shaken by what had just occurred, but no one more than Dan, Kyle and May. They knew it was no coincidence that they were the only people approached and questioned on that train.

CHAPTER 4

❧

Finding Zan

That evening everyone was talking about what happened on the train earlier in the day.

"What do you suppose they wanted?" asked one passenger in sleeping car number 27.

"I don't know," said another man, "Probably making a quick check of the train from outside."

Then why did they come inside? Who were they and what did they want?"

"It wasn't a robbery," stated another who stopped in as he was passing by and opened the car door.

"People don't just wear masks to hide their faces. If you ask me, that's not right and just plain not normal."

One of the two men seated in the car replied, "Well, Halloween is just around the corner, ya' know."

The man was now leaning against the car door, "Yea, well it's still strange."

When the train arrived in the town, Kyle and Dan waited for May outside. Back in Row 31, the family of three who had gotten to know May on the trip was concerned for her and her friends.

"Are you sure you and your friends will be safe?" asked the mother as she got her bag from the overhead bin.

"Yes," May said reassuringly. "We'll be just fine."

The mother then walked out of the car with her daughter as the father said to May, "You and your friends be careful now; those freaks from yesterday did seem to take interest in you."

May nodded her head in agreement; she too grabbed her backpack from the overhead bin. Exiting the car she caught a short glimpse of the child, still walking beside her mother, looking back at her. May stared back at the little girl and gave her a weak smile and a wave. A women's voice calling out her name softly made May jump. She turned around to look back into the sleeping car but no one was there. May blinked her eyes and she turned her head back towards the hallway of the train but the hallway was no longer there; it had been replaced by an image. She saw a little girl with long brown hair and bright green eyes running towards a woman who was crouched with her arms held out calling to the child "May, come on darling, I need to give you something."

May watched as the toddler climbed into her mother's arms, hugging her tightly. The woman beamed down at her child and brushed the hair out of the child's face. The mother was holding a necklace with a crescent moon attached to it. The little girl turned and lifted her hair as her mother fastened the clasp of the necklace around the girl's neck. Just then another girl approached the woman.

"Oh, there you are Dawn," she said, now smiling an even bigger smile as the second girl approached. She reached down, took the girl's arm and fastened a bracelet around her small wrist. Attached to it was a silver charm, and carved in it were tiny stars and the planet Saturn. The two girls were delighted with their gifts. The woman put the younger girl down and hugged both girls tightly. Dawn held May's right hand as their mother stood up and turned to walk into the distance with the two girls following closely behind her. The teenage May stood there watching as they woman walked away with her two children.

"Excuse me? Um, excuse me miss, you're holding up the line." said a man's voice from behind.

May turned and saw a man looking at her with a line of people behind him trying to see what the holdup was.

"Oh, I'm sorry sir."

May turned her head one last time to look down the narrow corridor, but the image was gone. She then made her way to the doors of the train that were still standing open, leading outside. When she met up with Kyle and Dan her head was down.

"What is it May?" asked Kyle, noticing her shaken look.

May looked at the two of them and shook her head and with an awkward smile.

"It's nothing. Come on, we have a mission to do, right?" Kyle then let May pass and take the lead. He looked at Dan, who just shrugged and hurried to catch up with May. Kyle caught up too.

"Hey, May, are you sure, cause Dan sometimes…?"

May stopped and looked over at Kyle "I told you its nothing, now let's go already!"

"OK, OK fine, sure!" Kyle said with his hands up, in a signal of stand back. Dan then let May pass again and he decided it would be best to follow with Kyle and give May a little space. They walked through the town of Requiem and May spotted a restaurant after a five-minute walk, she turned to the two boys. "I'm sorry," she said. "Look, there's a restaurant. Let's go inside for a break, I need to tell you something important."

The restaurant May spotted was called The Shack, and locals sat inside and out. Inside The Shack, Dan spotted an open table in the corner next to a window. After ordering drinks and food, May told them about what she had read in the paper on the train. When she finished she could tell Kyle and Dan were thinking about what she had said.

"Do you suppose those two weirdoes that were on the train last night are the ones in the woods outside of town?" asked Kyle.

"I don't know," May shrugged and said "That's not important now, what matters is that we must continue on with the first part of the mission."

Kyle looked confused. "I don't even know the first part of the mission," he said.

Before he could ask Dan, his eyes were closed with his elbows on the table and his head resting on his hands. Now he looked up at May who told him they needed to find a person in town named Zan. A waitress came with both their food and drinks.

"Well" said Kyle "We'll look for this so-called Zan later. And besides we can't look for something on an empty stomach, right?"

Dan shook his head "You are such a dweeb sometimes, you know that?"

Even Dan knew Kyle was right even though they had not eaten anything since yesterday afternoon. After eating, May left the money for the food and drinks on the table. Walking towards the door, Dan asked where they should start looking.

"We should ask people around town if they know a person named Zan," said Kyle. May looked at him, took out her spell book, and hit him on the head.

"We can't just go around asking everyone we see. We have to ask people like us, remember? If you were paying attention while the Mistress was talking she said he wouldn't be hard to find since he's an unusual character in this town."

A man who was sitting at the nearby bar overheard them talking, stood up and walked over; the man caught Dan's eye.

"Did my ears deceive me or did I hear you youngsters talking about someone named Zan?"

May looked at the man whose eyes looked like he hadn't slept in weeks; he was wearing jeans and a jacket with sandals which seemed rather odd given that is was so chilly outside.

"Yes, sir, we were," she replied. "Do you know Zan?"

The man chuckled. "Of course, why almost everyone here knows that man."

May exchanged looks with Kyle and Dan, "Do you know where we can find him?" Dan asked.

The man nodded and led them outside and pointed towards a neighborhood ahead of them.

"You'll be able to find Zan in his house over there; if I recall correctly it's the one with the black roof."

Kyle and Dan started walking towards the house. May thanked the man for his help and went to catch up with the group as they heard the man shout, "Get there before dark!"

To be certain, May, Kyle, and Dan asked a few more people around town to see if what the drowsy man told them was true. Somewhat to their surprise, everyone they asked gave the same answer and directions to where Zan would be. At the entrance of the neighborhood was a torn sign and scraped on it were the words "Welcome to Hill's Peak." They started walking around. It was now dusk, the sun was going down and the gas streetlights in the center of town were already lit; some of the houses had their lights on too. In the windows were either children or someone standing there and as soon as they saw the three of them they would quickly rush to close the curtains, and turn off the lights.

"That's strange, wonder why they're doing that?" asked May. Kyle stopped walking and stared at a house just in front of them.

He shrugged and said, "I think that's the house," he said. They saw a house that looked exactly as the drowsy man had promised. All of the other houses looked exactly the same; two colors, peach and orange. But Zan's house was different, and it finally came to them. Upon seeing the house, they understood how almost everyone in the town knew Zan. The house in front of the group was painted blue with the chimney and roof painted black; it was an odd pairing of colors for a house. The curtains at the windows were slightly torn and were blue with wavy markings stitched on them. The house also had iron gates and at the top were gargoyles on each side, in sitting positions, glaring down at them. Kyle looked at the houses around them and back at Zan's and then to May and Dan, then back at the house and said, "Well, um, he's a bit eccentric don't you think. Ouch!!" Dan had smacked Kyle on the head with his right hand and walked over to the house followed by May. The sun was no longer in the sky; it was now night. The gates were unlocked, so Dan opened them and went over to the front door. Approaching the door, Kyle noticed a scratched out symbol as he began to knock. The lights were still on inside, but they were quite dim. Once more Kyle knocked, and then Dan saw someone's shadow moving past the curtains inside. Kyle took out his spell book. May was taken aback at his plan to enter.

"You can't just break in," she said, lowering Kyle's stretched out hand.

"He's in there alright, he just wants us to stay out here," said Dan. Before Kyle could use his spell book, the door opened slowly and they walked inside. The door closed behind them as Dan looked around.

"So who's this Zan guy anyway?" A light came on upstairs and a gaunt man with thinning hair in his late thirties stood before them.

"That would be me," said the man in a slightly accented tone as he came down the stairs. "Why are you three here? Lost or something? You shouldn't be outside at night you know with the reports of strangers in the mountain near here; the police have implemented a new curfew and are taking in people who are out at night for questioning."

Kyle was about to protest and then Dan stepped toward the staircase.

"We are here from the small town called Misty Road, and…"

Zan came down the staircase; he was tall and seemed to be a little out of shape. He walked passed the kids and into a living room. He made his way to a door and stopped.

"I know where you're from but that wasn't my question." He waved his hand and murmured something to the door and it opened. Inside was a rather small library and Zan stepped inside and closed the door behind him.

Inside the library Zan had his attention on one book that was sitting on top of a large pile.

"The Mistress sent us; she said you know her and the rest of the Academy's leadership." Kyle said through the door.

Zan looked down and murmured something, his thin brown hair slightly blocking his blue eyes. The kids heard him close a book and then the door reopened.

Zan closed the library door behind him, headed out towards the front door and said, "I suppose she wants me to return with you? So be it; let's go."

Kyle was as confused as Dan and May by how easy it was to persuade Zan to come back to the Academy with them. After closing the door and leaving the house, the four of them were headed back when two figures appeared from the shadows and made their way towards them. Zan and the rest quickened their pace as the two figures kept up with them. As Zan and the others started to run, Kyle looked behind and saw that the two figures were right behind them. Kyle, Dan and May reached the train first and were giving the tickets to the ticket man when Zan got to the doors. He opened the book he carried with one hand and stretched out the other and a brightly shining orb came beaming out, stopping their chasers in their tracks. After the train doors closed and the train took off, Zan gave the shocked ticket man his ticket and went over to the sleeper car where the three teenagers were. He opened the door, tilted his head forward since it had almost hit the doorframe, and sat down near the window.

"That was fun," he said, "Wake me when we get there." The ticket man stopped by their sleeping car and looked at them.

"Who are you people?" he asked as Zan made the door close on him with a wave of his hand.

CHAPTER 5

Back at the Academy

The train stopped at Misty Road. Zan, Kyle, Dan, and May stepped off the train as May used a memory charm on the ticket man before the train departed back towards Requiem. The walk back to the Academy was a long one and the whole time Kyle felt like they were being watched. Wherever he looked, he thought he saw something out of the corner of his eyes. May was wondering if Zan was as powerful a spell caster as Michael. When they arrived at the Academy, two counselors were waiting for them. One of the counselors grinned.

"Well, I don't believe it. Come back for a second chance, have we?" she said, greeting Zan as the other Counselor told Kyle and the others to go wait in the Mistress' office.

Inside the office, May told Kyle and Dan who she thought Zan was. They agreed that Zan must have great powers because he wasn't holding a wand, but he did have a book that looked similar to Master Michael's. In the hall they heard the voices of the Counselors and Zan headed towards the office. When they entered they saw that Kyle and the others were there too. One of the counselors told them they had done a good job and sent them off to their dorms.

Inside the office, Zan stood beside the door with his arms crossed. The Mistress sat up in her chair.

"It's been a long time Zan. How've you been?" she asked pleasantly.

"Just get to the point. Why you need me back?" Zan asked her impatiently.

"Nice to see you too," the Mistress replied with a sigh. She stood up and walked to a nearby window. She looked outside at Kyle, Dan and May, who were talking with fellow classmates on the way to their dorm.

"Listen, Zan. We need you back for an important task," she said with her light green eyes focused back on him now. "We need you to go out and search for the fragments of the crystal."

Zan snorted at the idea of the Mistress choosing him for this important task over any other members of the White Witches.

"You know I'm no longer one of you so why choose me over everyone else?" he spat with fury as one of the Counselors looked at Zan in disgust.

"Because you're the only one we know of at the moment who has a fragment! I would expect you to keep that in mind!" roared a man, obviously quite distressed.

Zan rolled his eyes and smiled at his protestor, "All the more reason for you to get a fragment of your own. That way you can be useful for once, Vain."

Vain grabbed Zan by his cloak and made a threatening fist. "Why you… I should just…"

"That's quite enough. Vain release him," the Mistress shouted. "Zan, Vain is right, you should know better than all of us that the clocks have been ticking ever since the fateful night when the Monks' attempt to guard the crystal had failed."

Zan sighed. He looked at the Mistress. "Fine. I suppose I owe you," he said as he turned to leave. Just as his hand touched the doorknob Vain stopped him.

"One more thing. The three who escorted you here will be joining you."

Zan stopped dead in his tracks. "You want to run that by me again, Vain?" Zan asked with gritted teeth.

"You heard him Zan," said the Mistress now staring through the window behind her desk. Zan couldn't believe what he was hearing. It was bad enough that he was chosen for such a dangerous task. Now they wanted him to take a bunch of kids along for the ride. The entire thing sounded totally ridiculous. He asked the Mistress if Vain was serious. She told him that he was completely serious and that the three needed to put all they learned throughout the years to the test.

"Come on, I'm afraid babysitting is not part of my jurisdiction," Zan said disbelievingly. "Or has the Council lost all its supporters and now requests this younger generation as a back up? How can we be sure that the council speaks the truth when they say they won't do anything when the crystal is formed?"

"Zan you're still dwelling on what happened years ago." Even though Tamara's voice was calm

Zan could tell he had gone too far. "You know better than anyone how bad things will get. And I do not wish for these students to suffer for our mistakes, but if it comes to that then we won't have a choice. Dark times lie ahead, Zan. And when the time comes again for choosing sides, will you have let go by then?" Zan rolled his eyes and walked over to the same window.

The Mistress reassured him that the kids wouldn't be a problem. The two saw Kyle through the window, telling everyone around him to back off. Kyle now had an orb forming in the palm of his hand and was taking aim at a nearby tree. He fired, but the orbs energy gave way. With a swoosh, the energy that was held inside the orb sent a shock wave back and knocked Kyle off his feet. His back hit the ground rolling him backwards. The group around him stared down at him. Some laughed and some gasped, hurrying to his side helping him to his feet. Zan shook his head with great disbelief. Even the Mistress closed her eyes and frowned with embarrassment.

"Oh yea, they're as good as dead against the Akolt," Zan said as he walked towards the door. Before he left he told them that he'd do it; not for his former members, but only because he owed the Mistress. His long stare of hatred lingered on Vain, Zan's eyes meeting his deep violet glare and then left abruptly.

The rest of the day passed with lots of questions for Kyle and his team by fellow classmates about how the mission went. At night everyone slept soundly in their dorms. Kyle awoke to the feeling of being watched. He got out of bed and walked over to the window, peeking through it. The moon was almost full and the light illuminated the grounds and trees outside. He could only conclude that he must have imagined it. Kyle then went back to bed and fell back asleep. Outside a figure emerged from behind a tall tree clutching onto a branch. The figure then released his grasp of the tree and wandered off into the night.

The next day Zan met Kyle and the others down by the trees and told them what the Mistress had told him and when he was finished, Dan was putting two and two together.

"So let me get this straight," he said "All of us are going with you on a big assignment starting the beginning of next week?"

Zan looked at Dan. "That's right, so get started on thinking about what you'll need, but don't pack a lot. You won't need much, just clean clothes suited for blending in, spell books and toiletries."

With that said, Zan told them to head off to class. He turned and went towards the main building. The three teenagers fled to their conjure class in a hurry, fearing that if they were late again Professor Shane would live up to his promise to turn them into roaches. In the classroom the bell was three seconds away from ringing. The door flung open. Dan shoved Kyle out of the way. Kyle's head hit the doorframe, allowing May to pass by gently. Just as Kyle was able to focus back on the classroom, the bell rang.

"Mr. Fang," said Professor Shane calmly; his partially bald head and squinty blue eyes popping up from a pile of books that he soon levitated to a nearby shelf. "Please close the door and get to your seat."

Kyle did what he was told. His seat was assigned at the table where Dan was already seated with another boy younger than they. Giving Dan a sharp look, Kyle was just about to sit down when Professor Shane called out to him.

"Mr. Fang since you are late to my class you know the penalty. Set your bag down first please."

Reluctantly; Kyle set his bag on the table and the short plump professor took out his staff and pointed it at him. The staff shot a yellow thread at Kyle making him shrink into an insect. It wasn't a cockroach. Instead Kyle was turned into a fire ant. However, for some strange reason the Professor's staff seemed to always misjudge logic and make things a little bigger than what they normally are. Dan looked down at ant Kyle.

"Well, at least it's not a cockroach."

"Spare me!" Kyle shouted back in a squeaky voice.

He began crawling to the foot of the table; to Dan it didn't seem far at all but to Kyle it was like hiking up Mt. Everest.

"Dan, help your friend get to the table so we can begin today's lesson."

Dan carefully held out an open arm for Kyle who crawled on. Once on the table Dan and the other boy stared at the ant. Dan looked at the curly red haired boy sitting beside him.

"So, David, how's your spell casting coming?" The boy looked at him shocked.

"You talking to me? That's weird, you never asked me anything before." he said, now getting out a book on conjuring orbs.

"Don't get your hopes up, David. He's just trying to make the best out of a tough situation," said Kyle in his squeaky voice.

"Oh, that's why. OK, I forgot. It is him after all," said David with a smile. Luckily for everyone, David was an easy person to get along with and hardly ever argued about anything. He was one of those people who looked for the positives of a situation instead of the negatives. Even in a troubling spot he tried to find a way to solve the problem instead of giving up automatically. The lesson was on summoning orbs to the palm of the casters hand and then controlling the energy flow so that it wouldn't give way and send the caster soaring backwards. For this lesson, they had to move all the chairs and desks from the middle of the room. When Dan finished moving the table over, the fire ant Kyle crawled onto his hand and bit him. Dan gave a quick shout of pain as the fire ant leapt off and stared into his eyes.

"That was for shoving me into the door when we walked in." he squeaked. The Professor looked at the fire ant and took out his staff. Kyle was transformed back to normal, but had a slight feeling of lightheadedness as he stood.

"That will wear off eventually," said Professor Shane happily. "Come Mr. Fang, demonstrate for us what conjuring an orb looks like."

Kyle trembled a few times before his feet regained their balance. Sneaking a look at Dan, he opened his book to a page with an illustration of two shaded figures. A man and woman were in a stance with their right hands stretched out and an illustration of a shaded orb hovering inches above their palms. The instructions indicated that the caster must pass as much energy as possible to the palm of the other hand. The demonstration underscored how critical it was to focus the energy in order to control the strength of the flow once the orb was formed.

Kyle walked to the center of the open space, copied the stance, stretched out his right arm and opened his hand. As he concentrated for a few moments, light blue threads started to form out of his palm and rotate clockwise. Faster and faster the threads spun until a light blue orb was hovering in the palm of his hand. The professor laughed with excitement and told Kyle to focus the energy so that he'd be able to control how powerful it could become. Kyle focused for two minutes but after that the orb's energy faded.

It poofed out of sight and sent a shock wave through Kyle's right arm that knocked him off his feet and to the ground again. The students in the room all gasped. Several rushed over to help Kyle get back up. Professor Shane nodded his naked head.

"Well, not a bad attempt. Everyone take turns now. I don't want any accidents so be careful."

Everyone formed groups of two. One conjured orbs while the other was the spotter, then they switched places. The next classes that day were on levitating objects that were out of reach and opening objects that had a strong sealing spell on them. The whole class had difficulties with the task and had to take their incredibly well-sealed objects with them to finish in their dorms for homework. The last class of the day was in Laws of Magical Creatures. The topic was the moon's cycles and werewolves.

"Excuse me Professor Taylor, sir, I always thought werewolves were just a folk tale," said a student sitting at a desk beside David. Professor Taylor stopped drawing the moon cycles on the chalkboard and looked at her with serious eyes. He swooped over to her desk like a bat and she grew silent.

"Really… did you now?" he asked in a low rough voice.

Professor Taylor was a tall, thin, dark skinned man with matching jet black hair whose eyes seemed to be like a hawk's, never missing a thing that happened in his classroom or anywhere else at the Academy. His face had signs of facial hair everywhere except near his gray eyes that had deep black eyelashes.

"Well, Kate, that question must remain unanswered, until one finds out for oneself," he said curtly. Kate lowered her head, letting her light blond hair run down her face. Kyle was passing a shriveled up piece of paper over to another classmate to his left when the feeling of a presence stopped him.

"Mr. Fang!" Kyle almost jumped out of his seat.

"I take it you find my class amusing in some way. Now dispose of that pitiful letter before I give both you and Collin a spot in detention again."

The lesson continued as everyone took notes on the professor's lecture. He also gave them writing homework on the day's lesson. The homework question was, "Do you agree or disagree about the mark of the wolf? Does it turn those who bear it into mindless beasts that aren't able to control their actions? Explain why or why not using the notes that you took in today's class."

After dinner, some students, both magic and mortal went to the school library to study, while others either went to the break room to play pool or simply relax before returning to the dorm to do homework or outside to play short sports games. Kyle, Dan, David, and Collin were setting up a game of pool next to another game that had just started. Dan got the pool cues and chalk while Collin set up the table.

"I'm telling you guys. Professor Taylor scares the hell out of me," Kyle said, taking a pool cue from Dan. Collin and David nodded in agreement. Dan closed his eyes with no comment, but somehow they thought Dan must have thought the same thing at least once in a while. Collin removed the triangle and took two sticks from Dan, keeping one for himself and sharing the other with David.

"Did you guys believe the lesson? On werewolves and all?" he asked, just to start a conversation.

"Nah, no way, it's a load of bull. Besides, if there were such creatures, you would think people would have killed them all. I mean really.

Seeing a huge hairy person with claws and fangs would be enough to give anyone the thought of killing them before they ran rampant," David said before asking if Kyle wanted to break in a game of nine-ball.

The teams of the match were set with Kyle and Dan against David and Collin.

"Well, there have been many stories about them you know," said Collin. "Like they say, every story comes from somewhere."

David raised an eyebrow, "I still think its crap." Kyle took a close look at every pocket in front of him, placed the cue ball in the center of the table and took careful aim.

"Guys, Professor Taylor doesn't give a damn if you agree or not, as long as you get the assignment done. That's all he cares about. Two ball, right corner pocket," he said, pointing the cue stick to the high side of the table.

He hit the white ball and sent it rolling towards the diamond of balls. In an instant, the balls were scattered across the table, but none fell. In the library May was finishing her werewolf assignment with other girls from the class, including Kate, who was silent the entire time.

"Don't let it get to you." said one of the girls sitting beside her. "We all know how Taylor is; heck he acts the same way around the rest of the faculty."

"Thanks, Myra." Kate said with a smile. They had just noticed the Librarian, Ms. Gil shutting the lights off. They packed up their things after Kate wrote down one last sentence and left.

Outside on the grass field students were finishing up their games and heading back up to the dorms just as the sun was going down. Kyle, Dan, Collin, and David were coming out of the break room. Their epic best two out of three games of pool ended in a 1 - 1 tie as they ran out of time. The sunset gave the scenery a soft look as if they were in a pleasant dream realm. The boy's dorm was three staircases up from the bottom and the girl's dorm was yet another three staircases up. Inside their dorms there were doors on each side of a long hallway. Each room had one or two bunk beds, two big chests of drawers for clothes, and a sink. Kyle shared a room with Collin and a mortal ninth grader named Richard.

Kyle was struggling with his small sealed case for the seal opening class while Richard studied for a history test the next day. Since the mortal students in the Academy shared rooms with the spell-casting students, the mortals followed strict rules both in and out of the Academy. Most importantly, it was understood by all that one should never tamper with anything that belonged to the spell casters. Collin walked into the room brushing his wet blond hair out of his eyes. Kyle and Richard then knew that Collin had washed his hair in the sink by the dorm bathroom. He then got to work on his sealed chest, taking out a piece of parchment that had writing on it. He placed it on his chest but noticed Kyle still struggling.

"Richard, you think you mortals have it tough? You don't have to do this crap. Open, damn you!" he shouted, removing his hands and then placing them again on top of the small case.

"Yes, 'cause it's every mortal's dream to shout at inanimate objects and be just like us." said Collin with a raised brow.

He noticed Kyle's piece of parchment on the floor and said, "This might come in handy."

Kyle took the paper, looking embarrassed.

"I knew that." he said putting the parchment on the small case and placing his hands over it again. This time he broke the spell and opened the small case easily. He then placed it aside and took out his werewolf assignment. Soon after, Collin was also able to eliminate the spell from his chest and open it. The two finished their other assignments a few minutes before time for lights out.

CHAPTER 6

꧁꧂

The Fragment, the Dream

It was the last few days before Kyle and the group was to leave with Zan. Saturday afternoon in the Academy was erupting with conversation among the spell casters. Outside the Academy, David ran over to Dan who was reading his book on mythology. Dan's eye caught David. He closed his book and noticed the worried expression on David's round face as he caught his breath.

"Dan… I have a… big problem. I can't find my spell book."

"Did you look in your room?" asked Dan.

"Yes. I think someone took it."

Dan looked disbelievingly at David, crossed his arms and started to think.

"You're kidding. Who would take... wait don't tell me, follow me." Dan stood up and led David to a group of mortal kids who had passed by Dan earlier and were now crowded around someone or something on the ground. The crowd of little kids watched as the two cleared the way. On the ground was a little girl who clutched a book tightly to her chest. Her eyes had gone blank as she gazed up at the sky. She wore a green shirt and pink shoes. Her long hair was fanned out across the ground. Dan dashed towards her; he knelt down and examined her closely. He then opened his spell book and flipped through the pages. The page he turned to was a spell on counter curses. With an outstretched arm he placed his free hand on the girl's arms, which were crossed over her chest.

A few seconds later red threads slowly appeared and wrapped around the book the girl was clutching. She released the book instantly and her eyes returned to normal.

"What happened?" she asked, getting up slowly and gazing around at everyone.

"You tampered with something out of your control," answered Dan seriously. He stood up tossed the book at David who caught it.

"I didn't mean to," she said in a hoarse voice, "The fifth graders said nothing would happen…"

"Really, would one of the fifth graders name be Charles?" David asked. The little girl, who was now crying, nodded as she rubbed the tears from her eyes.

"Figures," David said through clenched teeth. "The next time they tell you something like that, don't believe them."

The little girl nodded again. This time she ran off with her friends following close behind. One of the little kids thanked Dan and then ran to catch up with the rest of the group. Dan turned to leave; David followed close behind. Once back on the other side of the Academy by the grass field, David remembered what he needed to tell Dan before his book was taken.

"Dan, before I forget, I need to tell you something. Starting next week your group isn't the only one with a new assignment. Everyone is going to learn new things about spell casting at some point. I don't know why though."

"You mean to say no one gave an explanation?" asked Dan.

"No, no one. And I suppose that Zan guy didn't tell you why your group is going with him either, huh?"

"Not a hint." Dan replied.

The two had a sickening feeling in their stomachs whenever they thought about the new plans for the Academy. What made things even worse, was that Dan and his group might not be around long enough to find out how the changes would impact the school. Lunch in the cafeteria was as noisy as ever as students talked excitedly about anything that caught their interest. At one of the occupied tables, Kyle was arguing with Collin where Kate and several others also sat; Dan was called over by Collin.

"OK, he won't listen to us, so you reason with him."

Dan sighed and asked why. Kate told him that Kyle planned on sneaking into Zan's temporary housing near the campus that night before they all headed back up to the dorms. The reason for this ridiculous idea was that Kyle wanted to see what was in Zan's spell book that was so important that he kept it locked away at all times. The girl started trying to talk Kyle out of it again and then grew silent as Professor Taylor walked by with his tray of food. He stopped to stare at them for a brief moment, his shiny gray eyes glaring at them, and then proceeded to a nearby table where three other professors sat. Collin stared in shock

"Now I see why David thinks he's a Were...." He cut his thought short when he saw the look Kate gave him. Kyle looked at Dan who was just taking a bite of his sandwich.

"So how about it? You in or not?"

Dan swallowed and shook his head. "As much as I would like you to get me into trouble again, I don't feel like getting caught by Count Dracula." he said as he took another bite of his sandwich.

He then noticed Kyle looking down at his plate and using his spoon to fiddle with his bowl of Jell-O. Dan turned with his mouth full and saw Professor Taylor glaring down at him.

"That's three days of detention with me, Dan. Starting tomorrow in my classroom," he said curtly and walked over to get a spoon and napkin before heading back towards his table.

Dan glared at Kyle who said, "You couldn't have held your tongue for two seconds, could you?"

The rest of the afternoon passed with the appearance of May coming back from her dad's house, below the campus grounds. Kyle soon found out that Zan lived in the house next to hers. When she asked why he was interested, he told her not to worry about it and went back to a game of kickball. Shortly after the game ended Kyle's team losing, Kyle slipped off to sneak into Zan's house outside of the campus boundaries.

Kyle already knew where May's house was in the faculty housing area, so it wasn't hard to find Zan's. May's house had a blue roof and the house after that had a copper one. Kyle approached the next house and peeked through the window. May's dad saw him and called out to him.

"Oh, it's you Kyle. What are you doing down here at this hour?"

"Zan wanted me to put something in his house for him," Kyle lied.

"He's not home at the moment. Can it wait until tomorrow?" he asked. Kyle shook his head no, so May's dad somewhat reluctantly gave Kyle a spare key to the house and told him to be quick. The inside of the house was like May's; it had a fireplace and chimney. On the walls there were pictures of various places around the world. A couch sat under the picture window. A TV was on the far side of the room, and stairs led to a bedroom and bath on the second floor. The entire first floor was a living room and kitchen. Kyle then spotted a desk in the back corner of the living room; after examining the drawers in the desk carefully he found nothing. As he was pulling out the desk in hopes of finding something behind it, he saw a hidden drawer and pulled it open. He saw a black book and picked it up. A red ribbon was tied around it. In the center was a symbol of some kind that Kyle had never seen in any of the other spell books used in the Academy. Glancing around nervously, he untied the ribbon and opened the book.

On the inside of the cover page was a hole that held a glass container. The hollowed out area of the book which held the container was shaped in a fashion to hold something of a very precise, descript shape and size. Inside the container was an irregularly shaped fragment of some kind that somewhat resembled a chipped rock. Kyle tilted the container and poured the fragment out. He scooped it into his left hand and held it close lightly between two fingers to examine it. Suddenly he heard faint sounds from behind him. He turned and looked, but no one was in the house except him. The noises grew to what sounded like whispers. The more they grew, the clearer they became. The whispers were in a language Kyle had never heard before. The fragment became scorching hot and Kyle dropped it instantly, but the strange thing was that his entire hand felt like it was burned even though he had only held the fragment with just his thumb and index finger. The voices grew fainter and the fragment started to glow blood red.

Kyle cautiously scooped the fragment up, placed it back in the glass container, and returned it to the book where he had found it. As he slowly closed the book, the blood red light softly illuminated the room until the last pages covered it. He retied the red ribbon around the black book and left the house, clutching his left hand. Back outside, Kyle locked the door to the house and gave the keys back to May's father who was waiting for him.

"There you are boy. You better head back up before you get into trouble," he said as Kyle let his left hand go and gave the key back to him. Giving him a quick thanks, he headed back up to the Academy as May's dad gave him a curious look with his dark eyes. As he walked up the stairs to the boy's dorm, he kept thinking of the voices he heard in Zan's house. At the entrance of the boy's dorm, Kyle pushed open the doors. In the hallway of the dorm, a sickening feeling filled his stomach as his eyes fell upon Professor Taylor who was coming out from one of the Counselor's rooms. He stopped to look at Kyle and grinned.

"Ah, Mr. Fang, you just barely made it on time. Shame, just when I was looking forward to seeing you in detention with Dan." He then walked to the front doors of the dorm, pulled one of them open and walked out, letting the open door close on its own.

That night, while everyone else was sleeping Kyle was tossing and turning in his bed. Sweat was running down his face. In his deepest sleep, Kyle found himself running out of a wooded area and into the edge of a town. For some strange reason, it felt like someone or something was steering him to go in a very specific direction. As the dream continued, he found himself stopping in front of a house - the scenery that included shops and blackened roofs told him that he was in Requiem. Just ahead, coming out of a nearby bar, was a group of about fifteen people in black cloaks. He had just begun to follow them when the scenery went dark. He then found himself in what felt like a never-ending black curtain when a sudden feeling came over him. He wasn't alone; out of the shadows he started hearing voices, at first faint, then louder and louder.

"What the two fear most, they shall become!" Kyle turned around and saw a dimmed light and another voice started to speak from the direction of the light. "Find them. Find the fragments! The half breeds know. Find them all!"

There was a bright flash of light and Kyle woke up shivering uncontrollably and found himself staring at the window. It was raining outside, the wind was howling and in the distance he heard the crackling of thunder. Kyle rolled over so that he wouldn't be awakened by another flash of lightning. He slowly went back to sleep, only to his disappointment, this time he was dreamless.

CHAPTER 7

Leaving Friends

Dan's Sunday started off with the usual breakfast in the cafeteria followed by the long walk to Professor Taylor's classroom for detention. He gave Kyle a good long glare and left the cafeteria. In the halls of the building Dan saw teachers preparing for tomorrow's classes. Some were cleaning the chalkboards, some were stacking books in their proper place, and a few were even checking the desks for signs of cheat sheets since the mortals had tests in their science classes the following day.

Professor Taylor's classroom was on the next level up; the entire atmosphere in room D12 was unnerving to the students. It was as if the room itself was alive. Portraits of mythical creatures hung from the walls and a portrait of a griffin was hanging from the center of the classroom, its wings outstretched and soaring with pride in the sky. More paintings and portraits surrounded the room with their majestic themes - the most dazzling of all was an artist's interpretation of two different realms. One was like looking into a nightmare. It had dead trees scattered across the landscape, the sky was red and black with images of gusting winds; a depiction of dirt being picked up from the scorched earth added an extra touch of realism. The second interpretation was an entirely different realm, portraying a scene out of a good dream with clouds drifting above the endless grassy plains, scattered lazily across the sky. A lake was in the center which was more unimaginably blue than anyone had ever seen; the grasses were tilting which gave the sense that it was windy and even the lake had that same feeling of being moved by the wind.

Other portraits included Harpies, which were the most beautiful creatures, strolling in a snowy landscape; a group of Slavic's playing harps on the rocks of a bathhouse; and three Changelings sitting on the forest grounds near a tree, scavenging the ground for mushrooms. Every painting and portrait had its own story to tell. Dan kept making his way through each, totally awed by the appearances.

"Enjoying the works of art?" asked a cold voice from behind.

Professor Taylor stood at the classroom door in bit of a daze. He seemed tired for some reason; his eyes were only slightly focused as he made his way to the front of the classroom and sat in his rolling chair.

"Luckily for you, I'm in no condition today for detention assignments so feel free to roam around. Just don't go into that room," he said sharply, pointing at a door behind him in the right-hand corner of the room. He then took out a book from his desk and began reading.

"Sir, I have an assignment to go on with Zan and my group tomorrow so…." Before Dan could finish his sentence Professor Taylor raised his hand, commanding silence.

"So you won't be able to continue your punishment. No matter, it gives me plenty of days without you and your hooligan friends disrupting my class," he said in a serious tone and went back to his book.

Dan continued his stroll, taking long glances at each work of art, and later going back to the ones he liked the most. A half hour passed quickly; there were only 15 minutes remaining in his detention so he spent the rest of the time perusing books on mythical creatures. He turned the page to a picture of a werewolf and the page opposite of it had the moon cycle and descriptions about werewolf behavior.

Dan glanced over at Professor Taylor who was fast asleep; his head rested on his left hand with the book he had been reading sitting open on his desk. Dan's attention was immediately drawn to the door in the right corner of the room. He looked at the clock. Only 11 minutes remained; he might be able to take a quick look before the time was up. He gently pushed his chair out and as quietly as possible made his way to the door. He stretched out a hand to open the door. He pulled on the knob, but it was locked. Looking around, Dan's eye caught sight of a key on the professor's desk. He tiptoed over and grabbed it, went to the door and unlocked it. When he opened the door, it made a slight creaking sound. Dan poked his head into the room briefly, but the room was pitch black so he couldn't see anything; he glanced back at the clock. Only two minutes remained as he gently closed the door, relocked it and set the key back where he found it. He made his way over to the painting of the Harpies.

Professor Taylor awoke and rubbed his eyes. He spotted Dan starring at the Harpies and looked up at the clock.

"Time's up kid, get out of here." he said catching Dan's attention.

"Professor if you don't mind me asking; what is in that room over there?" Dan asked.

Professor Taylor looked at him suspiciously and now Dan wished that he hadn't asked that. "Nothing of importance to you, that's for sure," he said still looking at Dan in a way that made him feel more than a little uncomfortable.

"OK. Well, good-bye professor," said Dan, quickly making his way to the classroom door before Professor Taylor could stop him. Once outside, he remembered David's suspicions about Professor Taylor.

"Oh great; now I'm starting to see it," he thought to himself while walking down the hall. However, it would explain a hell of a lot if it was true.

Lunch in the cafeteria was followed with questions from the group about how the detention went.

"So did he make you write an extra long essay or what?" asked David

"Knowing the professor I'm sure he did," said Collin. "Well, out with it."

"He told me to do whatever I wanted to do during the time I was there. All he did was read and then sleep."

"Hmm. That's not like him. He never sleeps during detention." Dan mentioned that he saw how David might think the professor was a were-wolf. Collin crossed his arms and raised an eyebrow.

"If he is, they wouldn't let him teach us, let alone stay here. Would they?"

Kate shook her head. "If he is, the Mistress must trust him and the staff enough to put him somewhere when the moon is full so that he can't harm anyone."

After lunch they all they went down to the sports field to hang out and join in a game of soccer. As usual Joshua announced every move by both teams as he guarded his team's goal.

"Five minutes into the game Kyle's team has the ball. Collin passes one player and then another and kicks it to Will. Will has outsmarted Dan; Kate is now in the open, Will kicks the ball to her as she too passed William. Oh Crap!"

Kate saw an opening and faked a kick as Joshua dove. As he dove to his right Kate scampered to the left and shot.

"Goal!" shouted Will. Stopping in his tracks his turquoise eyes widened and arms raised high in the air as if he was being arrested. Dan went over to Joshua and helped him up.

"You might want to lay on the announcing and get your head in the game," said Dan. Joshua was a short plump kid who had dark hair and olive skin. Kate, despite her sour attitude towards sports, was a natural. They had all concluded that she only acted as if she didn't like sports so that she wouldn't appear to be a show off. She was a little taller than May and they stood up for one another on occasions. Will and William were new to their group. William had a reputation for being the campus reject that enjoyed playing pranks on the professors whenever he felt like getting a good chuckle and therefore spent a good deal of his free time in detention. He was shorter than Kyle with somewhat long brown hair and brown eyes. Like Dan, he too was also well known for defense spells. Will was a tall scrawny teen with short brown hair. Some thought that William and Will were actually twins even though they didn't look alike and the two were often mistaken for one another. Will, William, Kate, and Joshua were one year lower than Kyle and the other boys and girls.

The game ended in a tie thanks to Dan's sheer determination to not be beaten by Kyle. The sun was already getting ready to fall behind the hills and the group had about thirty minutes left before dinner; as was often the case, some used the time to shower and change in their dorms while a few of the girls played blackjack and the guys played a few rounds of Texas Hold-em.

"C'mon …I need a… Diamond, how the hell do I have such rotten luck!" roared William pulling at his hair, unhappy at the cards before him.

"I raise two," said Kyle sliding the chips over.

"I fold," William grumbled, scratching his dark hair, then threw his cards to the ground.

"Same here," said Will. Joshua was watching the game from the hallway couch. Kyle smirked and set three more chips in. Dan did the same.

"OK, on three," said Dan, holding his cards up to hide his face.

"Fine, you're on," Kyle grinned. "One, Two, Three!" As promised both showed their cards.

"No Freaking Way!" Kyle snapped, letting his cards drop to the ground as Dan beamed and laughed.

"Too bad, mate, you should've quit while you were ahead." Kyle scowled in the face of defeat and looked down at his cards then back up at Dan.

"I don't know how anyone can beat you in poker when you have such a strong poker face." They were interrupted when one of the Counselors stopped by to summon everyone for dinner in the cafeteria.

Conversations about what Kyle, Dan and May would be doing with Zan the next day were that night's interest among the tables. Ideas ranged from possible escorts for important items or persons to the usual messenger work. Not surprising, since every assignment given to each group was to be something of that measure. The Akolt would attempt to intervene, but for some reason they seemed to be more absent as of late, though the school staff and members of White Witches didn't dwell on it much. Collin noticed two of the group leaders were missing at the table where all the White Witches sat.

"That's weird. Trent and Kimberly aren't ones who disappear much," He said looking over at the table.

"They went with Master Michael on his assignment," said May. "I'm sure they can handle themselves."

Kyle was taking a bite of his mashed potatoes when he saw Professor Taylor walking towards their table. He seemed irritated about something. This was a side of him that they had never seen before; his strange expression of something like enraged fear was quite evident. His full attention was on Dan when Professor Taylor reached the table and looked down at him.

"What did you see?" he snarled. All eyes at the table were on Dan; several other tables stopped chatting to eavesdrop on the moment.

"I don't know what you're talking about Professor," Dan said hoping that the furious teacher would just leave.

"Don't pull any of that with me." He glared, sensing that all eyes were on him and Dan. Everyone had pretended to go back to their own conversations when he turned his head to look at the numerous spectators. "I'm going to ask you again. What did you see?" he hissed.

"I told you sir. I saw nothing," Dan said. Professor Taylor's knuckles turned white squeezing the top of Dan's chair with his right hand. Taylor noticed his grip and quickly released the chair.

"Very well, I'll take your word for it, for now." And with that he stormed out of the cafeteria.

Kyle looked at Dan curiously. "Jeez, you must have done something really bad to get him all worked up."

"OK, you know the door on the right corner of his classroom? Well, while he was asleep I kind of took a look inside."

Seeing the looks of shock from his friends, he told them that he wasn't lying about not seeing anything in there because it was too dark. May sighed and took a bite of her macaroni salad. When Joshua was finished eating, nothing, not even crumbs, were left on his plate. The kids continued their conversation while Collin was finishing up his pudding. After dinner, Zan was waiting for Kyle, Dan, and May outside. He waved them over. The three told their friends that they would meet them later at the library.

As Zan walked, he motioned for them to follow him to the side of the dorm.

"Listen. Tomorrow we leave, so I suggest you tell your families that you'll be leaving for a few days and then get packed. Don't worry; the Counselors already know where you'll be. We leave at 6:00 a.m. from the entrance to the school. One more thing; don't be late."

The three did as they were told and went to Kyle's house outside the campus grounds. Since Kyle was arriving unannounced and could see they had company, he knocked on the door and soon his dad opened it.

"Oh Kyle, what brings you and your friends here?"

When they entered Kyle saw that his mom and dad were having tea with May and Dan's parents

"I'm glad that you're all here together. We need to talk with you," said Kyle.

When they finished telling their parents what they were going to be doing, the adults sat on the couch letting the information sink in.

"So Michael isn't in charge of you this time, is he?" asked May's dad.

"No sir," answered Kyle.

"I see. So they're letting this Zan watch over you three?" Quiet overtook the house; it seemed like minutes until Dan finally broke the silence.

"Excuse me sir, but do you disagree with the Academy's decision?" asked Dan.

"Well I'm not fond of it, but...never mind, forget it. So how long will you be gone?"

"Don't know, Dad," answered May, "but we'll let you guys know when we have the chance, alright?"

It was silent again as the three sensed the pressure on the adults. Kyle's dad stood up and said very calmly, "So be it. If it's what the Mistress thinks is best, then go."

His wife stood up also, "Dear," she said, clutching his arm.

"I know," he answered, "But if the Mistress trusts Zan then we should too."

His wife reluctantly nodded her head.

"So does that mean we can go Dad?" asked May. He too nodded his head, followed by a nod from Dan's mother.

"Now you three be careful and do everything Zan tells you to. Understood?" said Dan's mom. When the three kids left Kyle's house, May's dad closed the door. "I wonder. Can the Mistress really trust Zan?" he asked, hoping for reassurance.

"Again, I say if she trusts him then we should too," answered Kyle's dad.

"I guess you're right, Jake. If she thinks of it that way, then I back her decision," said Dan's Mom.

"We all knew this day would come eventually, Emma," said May's dad.

"Agreed, Remsly. It's OK. Marge, they'll be fine," said Jake to his wife who nodded slowly. The parents sat in silence for a long time, each reflecting upon the fact that the day had come. Of course, knowing that this was their child's destiny did not make it any easier.

Back in their dorms, they got ready for the next day. They packed all that they believed would be necessary. After that was done, the Counselors in both dorms called for lights out.

The alarm went off in each of their dorm rooms the next morning at 5:30 a.m. on the dot; Collin threw a pillow at Kyle for setting his alarm clock for such an early time. One by one, they got up and got ready in their rooms. Why would Zan need all three of them along with him? Kyle wondered to himself as he was making last decisions on what to pack. It must be an awfully big assignment.

When they had their spell books, clothes and flashlights packed in their bags as planned, they met Zan at the school entrance of Misty Road. From there, they started the long walk to the train station. Zan stopped the group at halfway and shared a few things for his group to keep in mind.

"If you're traveling with me, there are a few rules all of you should follow. One: you will do what I say, when I say."

"Yes Mast ..."

"Alright two: you will not address me as Master, only by Zan and that's it. And three: if you want to practice using magic I suggest you do it when not around mortals. No need to draw unnecessary attention."

"Like you did when we were escorting you to the school," said Kyle. Zan shot Kyle an irritated look and nodded in agreement, only to grin at the others when Zan's back was turned and the four continued on their way to the tracks. Once there, the train was waiting for more passengers. Dan got in first, giving his ticket to the conductor, and then the others followed him onto the train.

As the train was a good distance away from Misty Road, a gray fog appeared in the road nearby. Three figures emerged from the fog. One of them was giggling like a child in a candy store. "I want that one."

"Very well," said another. "Are those the ones the Master wanted us to get rid of?"

The third looked into the distance where the train was headed. "Yes," said a woman's voice. She too giggled as the fog started to cover them. "I think it's time we pick up where we left off with Zan."

If the train ran late which was often the case, they would have to catch another train in Requiem to get to Willow's Den. Fortunately, everything was running on schedule this day. The train ride to Willow's Den was shorter than the ride to Requiem and the town was bigger. Shops and cafes were at the center of Willow's Den. Zan told Kyle and the others that they were going into the mountains but first he needed to meet someone here and suggested that they go shop for the additional materials they would need for the trip because all of them now knew they would be going into a cave. Dan spotted a shop called "Come Get Some." The sign had a carved pickaxe and sweater on it. Inside the store the merchandise was much sharper than the name; Kyle, Dan, and May found small lanterns, matches, and rope used for climbing. After they found what they needed they waited in line.

The cashier looked at the three of them and asked, "Where would you three be going with all of this?" He seemed to be the only one working in the shop and happened to be wearing a navy blue winter toboggan. Kyle paid for the merchandise. "To the mountains," he said.

The cashier looked at them with interest.

"Well don't get lost now, wouldn't be the first time," he said.

Dan looked at the cashier with a glare and took the bags with their purchases. "What did he mean by that?" Kyle asked when they were outside the store.

"Probably nothing, just trying to scare us," said Dan, "Hey! Where's Zan?"

They looked around but couldn't find him. Just then May saw Zan entering a café off to their right. She and the others went over and sat at an outside table, close to the café window. Kyle put his hand into his jean pocket and pulled out what looked like a little ball of wax.

"What's that for?" May asked Kyle as he pointed inside toward the elderly couple that was greeting Zan.

"He must know them," he shrugged. Dan knew exactly what Kyle was doing.

"Wouldn't it be easier if we just went inside and joined him?"

Kyle looked at Dan and snorted, "Like that's any fun. I'm tired of that guy and everyone else withholding information from us. Take a piece and place it behind your ear."

Dan looked at the small lump of wax in Kyle's outstretched hand and slid away a few inches. "I can't believe you're going to eavesdrop. And where did you get that, anyway?" he said looking at the lump as if it had just been pulled out of the garbage, a doughty rotted yellow color with bumps all around, and what looked like a strain of fuzz poking out of each end.

"It's a… I don't know what it is exactly, but William gave it to me. He said it should help if we needed to listen in on something important. Look, if you two don't want any, then I'll do it myself alright?"

Clearly annoyed, both Dan and May took a small piece of the wax roll and placed it behind their ears and leaned their heads against the wall. The alarm was instantaneous when they heard conversations coming from inside.

"Correct me if I'm wrong, but I thought the phrase meet 'alone' meant that we meet here without anyone else," said Zan.

The woman gave no explanation but looked at the man sitting beside her wearing glasses and smiled. "Just like your father. You have the same sense of humor."

"They did say you were one of the quiet ones of the clan," Zan said to her.

The waiter brought them all coffee. The man and woman took cubes of sugar and stirred them into the cups.

"So tell me Mrs. Wallis, is your husband still pissing off the clan members or has he been busy with more important things?" asked Zan.

Mrs. Wallis snickered. "He is known for speaking his mind."

Outside Kyle, Dan and May were still tuning in with great curiosity. May looked over at Kyle as if to say, 'this is such a bad idea.' Just at that moment they heard Zan speak again.

"Before we all head for the train, why don't the three of you come meet Mr. and Mrs. Wallis and we can continue this meeting on the train."

He was looking right at them, not amused. Kyle, Dan and May went inside, shook Mr. and Mrs. Wallis' hands, and headed toward the train. When the train departed, they were all sitting in one sleeper car; they had requested a car large enough to accommodate all of them this trip. The small towns in the surrounding area with which they shared the school were unique. Practically everything in the towns was out of the ordinary, and that is what separated them from the rest of the cities.

"You three need to hear this," said Zan; Mr. Wallis nodded and had everyone's attention.

"Now I'm sure you three have heard the story of 'The Crystal of Light' Yes?"

Kyle and Dan found it odd that May knew the story and they did not.

"I only know bits of it," said May. "My Mom would tell my sister and me bedtime stories like that all the time. But what does the story have to do with our mission? I had always believed it to be just another story that parents told their children,"

Mr. and Mrs. Wallis nodded at May then looked at Zan who had his arms crossed.

"The thing is," said Mrs. Wallis, "it isn't just a child's fable."

May, Kyle and Dan grew silent. To tell them why they were going to the mountains, the Wallis' knew they would have to tell them the complete story. Mr. Wallis began the legend of The Crystal of Light.

∾

CHAPTER 8

❧

The Legend of the Crystal of Light

Some twenty-five years ago, during the cold autumn months, a battle raged between two clans, the Akolt, also known as dark wizards and sorcerers, and a group called the White Witches. Each side used their magic for very different purposes. The Akolt used dark magic for their torturous deeds. The White Witches used light magic meant for everything good and pure. The war seemed like it would never end. As their war grew, a member from the each of the clans secretly met and created The Crystal of Light. It alone kept peace between the two sides as long as it was undisturbed.

Shortly after the creation of the Crystal, a meeting was held to decide who would be the caretakers of it; in the end the monks were chosen to take charge of the Crystal. They kept it in a sealed glass container and put it in a room deep underground, beneath the temples. There the room's door was sealed and inside the crystal remained, undisturbed and hidden from the world. One small group of the Akolt members was enraged by the outcome of their war and the decision for peace. They defied the warnings of the Crystal's power, vowing that one day the group's leader and his followers would reclaim the Crystal and the power for their own.

Mr. Wallis took a long breath and Zan was looking out the window. Mrs. Wallis wasn't speaking and Dan broke the silence by saying, "Well that's good. Isn't the Crystal locked away?"

Zan sighed. "Unfortunately not, the Crystal was stolen ten years ago by the Akolt and shattered during the ensuing battle when the monks tried to recover it. All that remained were fragments like this one," he said as he pulled out a big fragment that was shaped like a crescent moon.

They all looked at it as Dan's eyes widened and Kyle was beginning to put two and two together.

"So let me get this straight. We have to do something about the remaining fragments now," Zan nodded yes. The train began to slow down as they approached the next town "Luna's Burg."

"I guess this is where we part," said Mrs. Wallis as they all exited the train. Before separating, Mr. Wallis wished them all the best of luck and went on with Mrs. Wallis, disappearing into the crowd of people at the station. Zan looked ahead and saw that the mountains they needed to reach were closer now, but they still had quite a ways to go.

"Do you know what will happen when we start gathering the fragments of the Crystal?" asked May.

Zan looked at the horizon "Let's just say, we'd best get ready for a lot of challenges headed our way." When the group reached the woods, they heard what sounded like someone running towards them.

It was the same cashier from the shop in Willow's Den and the group knew then that he must have followed them on the train.

"Listen, I'm sorry about what I said back there." He was panting as he caught his breath. "My name is Ren," he said. "My sister and I got separated in these woods a few days ago; although she's very capable of taking care of herself, I'm still worried. I know it's not your problem but could you please look for her while you are there?" Zan looked puzzled.

"Believe me I looked, but I couldn't find her. She may have gone into the cave where you're going. No one goes there though and very few know that it leads to the coast." Zan gazed off into the woods.

"How do you know she's in the cave?"

"I just have a strong feeling about it," said Ren. "Please. I will pay you if that's what you want?"

"Look, the problem of the matter is not money," said Zan, but before he could finish May said from behind him, "You don't have to pay us. We'll be happy to have a look and if she is there, you can be sure we will bring her back."

Ren's gloomy face brightened a bit at this and gave May a bow of thanks and, as they were leaving, he told them that his sister's name was Christine. As the group headed off into the woods, Zan wasn't the least bit satisfied with this extra task and insisted to May that she shouldn't make empty promises without being sure that all would go according to plan. May had nothing more to say on the matter and remained silent for the rest of the way up. The hike up was long, the wind was beginning to pick up, and the clouds overhead were getting grayer, but Dan soon spotted an opening to the cave up ahead.

"That would be it," said Zan. The group ran over towards the cave and Kyle took out a lantern from his pack, lighting it as he went inside.

"Hey Zan, you know we're spell casters right? So, what are you?" he asked Zan as he cautiously approached a huge hole in the ground at the back of the cave.

"Same as you but in a different league altogether." Zan answered as he crouched down and dropped a rock into the hole. May looked at both Kyle and Dan.

"I wonder," she began to say as Zan dropped a bigger rock down the hole. This one made a splash loud enough for everyone to hear. "Do you think Zan is with a type of special task force?"

"Maybe," said Kyle "But I think it's best to expect anything from him until we know for sure."

Zan interrupted their whispered conversation by calling over to Kyle for assistance.

"O.K. kid, here's the thing. We need to get down there. Do you have anything we can use to shimmy on down?"

"Yea, I'll get to it right away," said Kyle who began rummaging in his pack and pulled out a long piece of rope, attaching it to the harnesses het had gotten when he bought the rope. Kyle tied it to a stone formation that he spotted at the lip of the hole, while using another smaller piece of rope for strapping.

"Well let's go, nowhere else to go but down." Seeing that the rope held Kyle, the others followed him and made their way down. Kyle reached the end of the rope but unfortunately they hadn't reached the bottom.

"Uh guys, we have a problem; this is the end of the rope."

"OK. That's the last time you decide to do something without thinking it through Kyle!" yelled Dan.

Outside in the howling weather three hooded figures emerged. The tallest eyed the cave with confidence. "I know they were headed in this direction," he said. Inside the opening of the cave, they entered and started looking around one of them took out a wand and waved it about. The tip gave off light instantly and they continued the search. He moved his arm to the left and then the right, illuminating the damp walls and ceiling. The light then shone on the very spot where Kyle had originally tied the rope. The hooded figure smirked with delight and approached the tied rope and took out a dagger. "This should be easy," he said as he crouched down and with a flick of his wand, the light went out. "Chrick!" the rope started to snap. The four down below were shaken when they felt the rope giving way.

"What the hell was that!?" Dan asked, catching himself. Zan closed his eyes and then opened them again. He saw that the rope wasn't even close to reaching the ground and the four of them were dangling in mid-air, not even close to the bottom of the cavern, yet all relying upon a single rope. Looking down he saw that this hole led to an underground lake below them. "Everyone brace yourself!" he shouted.

Then with a loud "Snap!" the rope holding the four broke. They fell down and down, finally they all hit the water of the underground lake, landing with a tremendous splash. Dan was the first to return to the surface, then Kyle, followed by Zan and May. "Is everyone alright!?" asked Zan

"Yes!!" they answered back, one-by-one. It was now pitch black and the lanterns were useless since the matches were all wet.

"So much for the torches." said Kyle as he drifted on his back and started to untie himself. Seeing they were OK, the others untangled themselves as well. While drifting Zan raised his right hand and a bright orb of light shot out from the palm of his hand and hovered around them creating light for the group.

"Did you see that?" said May to Kyle and Dan who were also eyeing the orb above them.

"Yea," said Kyle amazed. "You don't suppose he can teach us that?"

"Honestly, is that all you can think of now?" asked May heatedly. "Don't you see? This proves it. He is like us, only better."

"I suppose you're right. But can we get out of the water now? It's kind of hard to swim with heavy gear and cloths on," said Kyle.

May rolled her eyes and Dan began scoping out their surroundings. The lake seemed to be vast in size. The orb was now gliding swiftly over a small rocky bank.

"Swim to the rocks." Dan said as he led them to the rocky shore. As they swam the hovering light drifted back towards them and slowly moved in the opposite direction illuminating other parts of the lake. When they reached the shore Kyle noticed that over the years the rocks had formed into big steps that led to a camp. As the group climbed the staircase, their soaked shoes squeaked on the wet rocks. They all brushed their wet hair out of their faces. The water sloshed down their bodies and then slowed to a drip.

Once they got to higher ground Kyle told them that the rope they bought from Ren was guaranteed not to break. Zan took the cut rope from Kyle and examined it closely. "Perhaps it was defective?" said Kyle

"Not likely," said Zan. "Cleanly cut with no signs of thread sticking out. This is no accident." He threw the rope aside. Kyle desperately tried to grab it but it had already fallen into the lake and was sinking quickly.

"Is that a jug?" May asked when she reached the top of the steps. Kyle went over to check. Just as he began to scout out the rest of the campsite, a voice shouted out to him. It was a girl about the same height as Kyle. She wore a red shirt, an unzipped black jacket, a red winter hat and held an unlit lantern with her left hand. Her hair was shorter than May's.

"Who are you!?" she demanded.

Dan started to look around and heard rocks hit the lake from the hole they had just fallen through. Unfortunately, the cave they were in was perfectly formed for echoes.

"Your brother Ren told us to find you, Christine," said May.

Christine had eyes that looked like she was seeing right through them and they sensed she could tell if they were telling the truth. She walked towards them.

"I swear that brother of mine is too much of a coward to come find me himself. Sometimes I wonder if I'm the older sibling or if we're even related," she said with a sigh.

When Zan asked Christine where she had been, she pointed to a passage straight ahead. Christine told him that while she was exploring, she had seen something illuminating the darkness far ahead and when she turned off her lantern and moved towards it she wasn't sure what it was. Christine agreed to lead the way as long as they agreed to take her with them back to Willow's Den or to her parents in Guardian's Peak. When she turned her lamp back on, the orb of light returned to Zan's open right hand and when he closed it, the orb disappeared. Christine looked at the orb in amazement before it vanished.

"Oh, that's a nice trick. Are you a magician?"

The group was at a loss for words and knew that they would have to use a memory charm on her if she saw any more magic. After Christine put her pack back on, they followed her into the passage. Out of the hole in the ceiling three fog-like clouds came sweeping down past the lake and on to the campsite.

"How unfortunate" said the hooded man "I thought that would be the end for them."

"No matter." said another, "Just follow them and stay out of sight."

CHAPTER 9

୬୨

Race to the Coast

Christine led Zan and the others to an area of the cave where there were several different paths they could take; she followed the one on the left. Minutes passed; the walls were soggy with heavy crawling roots. They walked for several more minutes.

"Not much farther now," said Christine. She stopped at a dead end and cut off her lantern; all was dark until a sudden sparkle of light was seen.

"Here it is," Christine said as she walked to the shimmer, which was partially hidden in a hole in the wall. She reached inside and pulled out a fragment. They walked back out of the passage, and Zan took out his piece of the crystal. The response was instant: the two remnants began to illuminate and when Zan took his piece out of his glass container they immediately fused together. The group stared in amazement as a thin beam of blue light shot out of the fragment and pointed in the direction of the passageway they should take next.

"There must be more fragments at the end of the cave," said Dan excitedly. Christine was confused and just as she was going to ask them what all the excitement was about, a purple streak of light flew past them. The streak hit the wall behind them creating a burnt spot.

"What? A stunning spell!" shouted Dan.

"Damn! Time to go. Run!!!" roared Zan.

As he started off, the fog clouds headed towards them. They tried several spells which were deflected as they ran down the slimy corridors. They reached another area with three paths.

"We have to split up!" shouted Kyle as he dashed towards the one on the left. Dan took the one straight ahead with Christine, and Zan took the passage to the right with May following close behind. Figures started to emerge from the clouds of fog.

"Take whatever passage you want Thomas. Mizori and I will follow the one with the fragment," he said as they took the right passage. Thomas waited for a brief moment and then took the middle passage.

As Kyle reached the end of his passageway he saw a hole in the wall about four feet off the ground that created a crawl space. Inside the crawl space there were cracks that allowed the light of the full moon to filter through. The middle passageway circled around and led directly to where Kyle was standing.

"Who are they!?" shrieked Christine running beside Dan who was pulling out his spell book

"I wish I knew," he answered back. They reached Kyle who waved them over.

"There's no one behind me, how about you?" asked Kyle. His question was answered when another stunning spell zipped right past him. Christine looked for a faster way out and spotted the same big hole in the wall that Kyle had seen. The opening was partially covered with thick vines all around it.

"Over there!" she shouted

"Dan, think you can break through overgrowth covering that hole!?" Kyle asked as another stunning spell soared passed him. He too was now fighting back with counter spells. Dan rushed to it and opened his spell book, while Kyle held their attacker at bay with his own stunning spells.

"You got the way cleared yet!?" he asked.

Dan was making headway on clearing a path. "Almost got it; keep holding him off!"

The final hit was a success for both Dan and Kyle as Dan's spell cleared the way and Kyle's spell stunned Thomas, rendering his right arm useless. "Come on already. Let's go!" shouted Christine as she began climbing into the hole. Kyle and Dan quickly followed behind. The three began to crawl as fast as humanly possible. Christine had to turn off her lantern so that they could not be seen up ahead. She quickly stuffed it in her backpack. The only light they had were the glimmers of moonlight through the cracks in the cave walls. Finally Dan saw an opening at the other end. He was almost through the opening when he saw a glowing orb following; it was May and Zan. May was hiding on the side of the passage firing orange colored spells as Zan deflected the spells fired back at them. Mizori and Raphael's hoods slid off as they were attacking, revealing dirty and slightly long jet black hair. Zan fired at the attackers, and at the same moment the attackers fired back. The two opposing spells collided in the passageway sending small lightning bolts ricocheting and hit-ting the walls where Dan's head was peeking out.

"What the…" he said as another bolt almost hit him. One by one they crawled through the hole and exited, going to a spot where they wouldn't be hit by any more oncoming spells. Kyle got May's attention.

"Let's get out of here. We're not going to be safe here for long!"

A fog cloud came from the hole in the wall where Kyle, Dan and Christine had just exited. May shot another orange spell, hitting the emerg-ing figure directly in the chest and sent him backwards into the wall where he slid down and slumped to the ground. His hood slid off exposing his golden red hair. They ran forward through the passage and Christine ran passed Zan who shot another bright light out of his palm giving them just enough time to escape. Mizori emerged from the now disappearing light and she saw Thomas rubbing his head.

"Get up Thomas, you idiot! They're getting away!" He got up and followed close behind.

Up ahead Zan and the others could now clearly see the light of the full moon, they had made it out of the cave. The brush and roots surrounding the cave disappeared. They did not stop until it felt like they were out of danger. Zan stopped running. All of them were clutching their aching sides. Dan sat down next to a tree trying to catch his breath.

"I think this is where we rest tonight," Zan said. Even for Kyle this was too much. His entire time in the Academy, he had wanted to see and be in real combat.

"So this is what it's like to be in real combat, huh?" he said, finding a spot to sit.

"Welcome to my world," said Zan. Christine pulled her lantern out of her backpack and turned it back on. It was now calm and the sound of the wind rustling was the only sound. They all sat quietly, their thoughts on what had just happened.

"OK, I don't know what that was all about back there, but something tells me that finding me isn't all you came here for. What's with all the colored lights back there?" Christine asked as she caught their facial expressions.

"Yeah, well it's hard to explain," Kyle said. He looked over at the rest of the group hoping that they could explain.

"It's strange, but I knew something was different about you four when we met in the cave," Christine said.

Dan looked to May for support. She then asked Christine, "Do you believe in magic?"

Christine hesitated for a few moments, then her eyes widened. "You're telling me that all of you are some type of magic people."

"So you do believe?" said Zan looking at Christine.

"Well, I have never thought much about it. My parents would tell my brother and me stories about it though. I guess they aren't just stories after all," she said. Kyle sat back against a tree trunk.

"Seeing is believing, I guess," he said as the rest of the group was settling in for the night near the fire Zan had made and Christine asked them what it was like to be a spell caster.

"Being a spell caster takes a lot out of you, even casting a simple spell uses up energy," said May who was now getting her water jug out of her pack. Zan was looking at the fragment that was still emitting a beam. Like a compass it was pointing straight ahead.

"So that's what happens when you put the fragments together," said Dan. Zan nodded. The next day they would have to go to the coast to search for the other fragments.

"There's more to the story of the Crystal than Mr. Wallis told you," he said to them.

Christine looked at them all, "The only story I know of a Crystal is the one my great uncle told my brother and me when we were little. Legend has it that if the Crystal ever broke, whoever put it back together would have control and the ability to decide the fate of their enemies. I guess the legend is true after all."

Zan nodded. Kyle, Dan and May were at a loss for words. Not only was the quest going to get more dangerous, but it was now imperative that they find the remaining fragments before the Akolt and put the Crystal back together. Christine also got settled for the night and found a good spot for resting.

"Those three that were after us were sent by the leader of the Akolt. Their names are Raphael the one with jet black hair, Thomas the golden red head and the one with dirty hair is their leader Mizori. They're only the beginning of our problems. We must be prepared for anything now," Zan said to all of them. With agreement all-around, the fire snapped and crackled as they all drifted off to sleep. They were exhausted.

CHAPTER 10

Fragments in the Sand

As night gave way in the mountains, the courageous group awoke to the smell of soup made by Dan; they ate, changed into the last dry clothes that had been wrapped in oilcloth and started off again. Arriving at the coast, May and Christine looked out at the waves of the ocean on which the rising sun created an unusual orange stripe. The white sand was pristine and undisturbed. As Zan took a couple steps forward, the fragment he had removed from the container was giving off the same blue beam that it had the day before. As the beam pointed down at the sand in front of him, he stopped. The group gathered closely around and began looking in the sand. Unbeknownst to them, up above them on the hill, a hooded figure with a leather mask gazed down upon them before fleeing back into to trees. The strange trio of Mizori, Raphael and Thomas were looking around the area where Zan's group had spent the night. Christine had forgotten her lantern in their rush to get to the coast. Raphael's eyes looked down at the lantern and kicked the it against a nearby rock, shattering the glass. The hooded figure got their attention. Raphael spotted the masked figure as it returned for the report on its patrol.

"The interlopers have found the location of the fragments," Raphael said to Mizori with great confidence. They quickly dispersed into clouds of fog and zoomed off following the mute masked figure.

The sand stretched for miles and the group searched rock to rock and even near the hillside. Christine saw for a brief moment a sparkle in the sand when the sunlight hit a nearby rock.

"I think I see it!" she called over to the rest.

May went over to where Christine was pointing. There they were, three fragments were partially exposed, lying beside the rock, their tips slightly sticking out of the sand. She went to scoop them up, but an invisible shield prevented her from touching them. May started to murmur words under her breath. When she had finished, she tried grabbing them again. The shield was still there, but her hand went through it. She quickly picked them up and carefully brushed the sand away. The reaction was like the last fragment found in the cave. The new ones instantly attached together to form a more robust fragment.

"Good work!" Kyle called over to her. "Now get back here so we can find out where to go next!"

May turned back and was running towards them, when a barrage of stunning spells shot out of the hill above them and hit the sand. Christine and Kyle went to her aid as a Prowler came leaping out of the grass behind them, landing directly in front of May. Both Kyle and Christine backed off and saw that a silk mask hid its face. Kyle knew that it was one of the same figures that boarded the train on their previous mission.

"Who is that Zan?" yelled Kyle. Zan was in a state of shock.

"A Prowler! Watch yourselves when you're facing it head on."

Kyle pulled out his spell book from his pack and tossed the pack aside. He shot a stunning spell from his hand it was met head on by another stunning spell. This sent both spells in opposite directions, as three fog clouds swooped down from the hill and landed alongside the first Prowler.

"It's them!" shouted Dan as he and May were pulling out their spell books. Zan pulled both a spell book and a wand from his bag.

"So that's what he meant when he said he was in a different league." Dan and May thought to themselves eyeing the wand and spell book. Two more Prowlers sprang off of the hill and all three turned into red fogs, dispersing and leaving only Mizori, Raphael and Thomas standing with their spell books and wands in their hands.

"Oh great, we're seriously out of our league here; only Zan has a chance," Kyle thought to himself. Dan was eying their spell books that had a pentagram on it just like the one on Zan's book.

"Wait! Doesn't that mean he's one of them, or was at one point...?" Dan thought to himself.

The Prowlers were sure to return. He and Kyle would have to fend them off while Zan handled the other three who had cut May off from her group. The boys had to time this perfectly as they'd only get one chance. Kyle looked at Christine.

"Get ready to run, OK? Now!" Simultaneously, Dan, Kyle and Zan shot their spells at Mizori's group who all countered with their own spells. Sparks flew everywhere when the waves of magic collided and the three Prowlers leaped out from the hill again. Dan and Kyle quickly turned and May made a break for it while protecting the fragments. Mizori's group was busy fighting Zan. The other two boys shot green colored spells at the Prowlers, each hitting its target and sending them hurdling backwards against the hillside. This caused them to turn back into red fog and retreat.

"I thought these guys are supposed to be hard to beat. They may look tough but they're just a bunch of cowards," said Dan.

Raphael caught sight of May fleeing down the beach and went after her.

"Give me the fragment!" he shouted while sending spell after spell at her. Christine came to her aid and shoved her out of the way as a stunning spell hit her on her side. She fell on the sand, motionless and Thomas looked at Raphael.

"You idiot! Be gentle with the one carrying the fragment. We must have it." One of Zan's two spells hit Thomas on his stomach and shoulder making him hit the sand with a loud thud.

"Enough of this!" Mizori barked as he struck May with another spell which made her knees give way.

She too was now lying on the sand motionless. All three Akolt rushed to the side of the two bodies and, with a smile, Mizori turned to fight Zan, Kyle and Dan. Raphael and Thomas crouched down beside the two girls and placed their hands on them and, and just before they disappeared into a fog, Mizori took the fragment from May and shouted with triumph in her black eyes, "Just try and save them now, Zan. We'll be waiting at the old house in the woods where it all began. Jeremy is waiting for us to return."

All that remained was May's spell book; Kyle went over to pick it up. "This isn't good. We need to get out of here," Zan thought to himself as they were left alone. He took all the spell books and put them in Dan's pack, picked Kyle's pack up and put them both on his shoulder along with his. He dragged Kyle over to Dan, and put his hands on their shoulder. In an instant they too turned into light red fog and vanished.

∽

CHAPTER 11

❧

Memories that won't be Forgotten

When Kyle woke, he was on a bed near a window. They were back in Willow's Den. At the foot of his bed he saw Mr. and Mrs. Wallis having a conversation with Zan. Mr. Wallis was pacing back and forth across the room, his light blue eyes nervously looking at every corner through his glasses.

"This isn't good at all Zan. If he has already sent out Mizori and her group, they must have more fragments of the Crystal than we thought."

Zan was sitting near the window looking outside and realized that Kyle was awake. "I agree, they must have found some before us."

"Kyle, if you and Dan want to head back to the Academy, I will understand; really, it's fine with me."

Mr. and Mrs. Wallis turned their heads to look at Kyle as he got out of his bed. As he started to rise, he felt extremely dizzy.

"It's perfectly normal dear. All first time spell casters who go through teleportation are likely to feel that way," said Mrs. Wallis as she headed downstairs. Kyle then crouched down and Mr. Wallis gave him a bucket to throw up in. Zan was still looking through the window where it was now dark and raining. Dan awoke a few minutes later and Kyle gave the bucket to him. Dan was immediately nauseous and threw up as well. Kyle looked at Zan

"We're going with you to get May and Christine back."

Zan sighed; it was clear there was no point in arguing with them. Mrs. Wallis returned from the living room and wanted to know who else was there other than Mizori's group. Zan looked at her.

"Jeremy has come along with Mizori."

Mr. and Mrs. Wallis looked even more worried. "Jeremy? The boy who attacked the temple?"

said Mrs. Wallis, her honey-colored eyes seeing the look on Kyle's face. She glanced back at Zan.

"Yes, the same," replied Zan.

Kyle was about to ask, but then Mr. Wallis cut across him. "Perhaps it would be easier if we showed them."

Zan nodded in agreement. Now Dan was standing.

"Zan. Kyle and I are going with you whether you like it or not." Zan nodded as a slight chill went down Kyle's back. They agreed to wait until the rain stopped to go to the old house in the woods. Zan took out his wand and placed the tip to his temple. As he pulled the wand away, he mumbled a type of healing incantation. Another strong chill went through the house, and then to Dan and Kyle's surprise the room was turning blurry. In a matter of seconds everything was gone, replaced with an entirely new setting. They were in a cemetery, dark clouds hung above, threatening to shed heavy tears. Crowds of people with umbrellas were walking by as if the group wasn't even there; a businessman walked right through Kyle and continued his stroll.

"Wait! How can they not see us?" Dan asked of Mr. Wallis who was standing by him.

"Because to them we're not even here; we might as well be ghosts of Zan's memories," said Mr. Wallis. "Let's proceed."

They walked over to a boy who was about nineteen that was staring at a large tombstone. The inscription read: "*RIP - Mr. and Mrs. Vane*" The boy started to sob and a younger Headmistress put her hand on his shoulder for comfort.

"It has been five years since the Crystal was given to the monks." said Mrs. Wallis, frowning. "A lot were lost then."

Behind the young Headmistress stood a much younger Mr. and Mrs. Wallis; they too were in tears. After the funeral, the young Jeremy stayed behind. As he stared at the tombstone, a figure approached him.

"Seems the protection of the Crystal is more important than their own lives." said a short plump man.

He wore a black suit with dress shoes and a tie. He also wore a black hat and had an umbrella at the ready. Jeremy turned to the man and glared.

"They were following the vows of secrecy," he said, his voice becoming hoarse. The plump man nodded and raised an eyebrow.

"Of course they were my boy, but see where that got them." It was as if the young Jeremy could see what the man was thinking; he grew cautious.

"Who are you and what do you want?" the plump man beamed at him and raised his free hand. "It's about to rain. If you want to know come with me, and you will have your answers and more."

Jeremy cautiously approached the man, who placed his arm over his shoulder and led him off into the distance.

"Zan," said Mr. Wallis.

"I'm on it." said Zan crouching on his knees. As he placed a hand on the ground, magic started to flow through it. The image of the cemetery grew blurry. And moments later, they were in some sort of temple grounds. Mrs. Wallis started to head towards the balcony of the temple. Zan stayed behind while Mr. Wallis went with Mrs. Wallis, Kyle, and Dan. After climbing the stairs and reaching the balcony, they saw a hooded man with his eyes focused on the horizon and two more figures appeared from the temple halls.

"Jeremy, the forces of Darkness are growing stronger with every passing day, soon they'll come for us," said one of the figures. Kyle looked into the familiar eyes. It was a younger Zan; his expression was one of worry and concern. This Zan was even thinner than the gaunt man they knew.

"I know," said Jeremy, frowning as his greasy blond hair shimmered in the sun light. "Have you decided what path you're taking?"

"Of course I have!" Zan shouted, his voice now filled with anger. "Surely you're not considering joining those traitors?" Both young men stood motionless there, the tension rising.

"I'm considering all options." Jeremy said calmly. "Let me ask you something. When the time comes to decide what path to follow, what will you choose?"

The younger Zan took out his wand and pointed it at Jeremy, his hand shaking.

"Don't even consider that option." protested Zan hoarsely. "If I must I'll do it. You're like a brother to me."

The younger Jeremy smiled wickedly at the young Zan.

"Do us both a favor and put that wand down before someone gets hurt. You don't have what it takes, you fool."

The second person raised her wand and pointed it at Jeremy, her hand completely still while her sapphire eyes focused only on him.

"If he won't, I will." she said sourly. Jeremy nodded at her and started to walk toward them.

"Stay back Jeremy!" she shouted, casting a stunning spell that hit the ground near his feet. "The next one won't miss! Stand down!" The two started to back up and Jeremy continued forward, unfazed by the threats. The two protestors were near the temple wall; Jeremy was now at the entrance hall. He looked at them, his emotion blank, his eyes darkened with rage.

"Just as I thought, Ana, you're just full of it. If you two want to become the best then join me; if you don't I won't have a choice the next time we meet."

With that he continued walking through the halls of the temple.

"What just happened?" asked Kyle.

"It appears that, over the years Jeremy grew dangerous to be around," said Mr. Wallis. "The Council kept a watchful eye on him, but could have never guessed that he would become what he is today... an Akolt member; poor Jeremy, he had such promise."

The image then became fuzzy again and a new image appeared. It was night outside; the temple was now under attack and parts of the ground and trees around the temple were in flames. The monks fled for their lives as crossfire appeared around every corner. The Prowlers caught sight of the horrified holy men and chased after them. Kyle knew they wouldn't make it. Killing curses went straight through Dan and Kyle's chest. The spells hit two White Witches, sending them tumbling down to their imminent deaths. Their attackers were a man and a boy.

"Nice one boy," the man roared with delight, "You may prove to be useful to us after all!" he said as the two quickly began dueling with more approaching White Witches.

The intense battles continued around the temple grounds and inside four White Witches were holding off seven Akolt members at the stairs. As spell after spell was cast, sparks flew around every corner of the temple and the windows shattered around the fearless fighters. Kyle and Dan were still on the balcony with Mr. and Mrs. Wallis watching the copper-haired Ana and three White Witches hold off four Akolt members. Ana dodged a killing curse and countered with a disarming spell. Success! As one Akolt's wand shot out of his hand, a warlock had magic flowing through his hands and finished him off with a burst of magic that knocked him off the balcony and sent him plummeting to the rocks below.

Countless Akolt members and Prowlers who appeared soon overran the four heroic defenders from the halls of the temple and from behind the balcony. A magical shield protected them for only a short time; several shield-breaking spells were launched and the four quickly went back-to-back, keeping their attackers at bay. It didn't last. It seemed that no matter how many attackers they stopped, more stepped in to take their fallen comrades' places. A Prowler leaped through the crowd and a dagger grew out of a vein in its hand and stabbed one of the four in the abdomen. His eyes were staring in disbelief at the Prowler's silken mask as it snarled in return and yanked the dagger back out of him. The wounded warlock fell to his knees and the Prowler lifted its hand up, the dagger covered in blood shining in the moonlight overhead. With one swipe, the dagger skidded across the man's neck and he fell to the ground dead, blood spewing.

"No!" one of the man's comrades shouted as she took her eyes off the attackers and looked at her dead friend. A killing curse hit her in the back, but refusing to give up, she gave a battle cry. With both hands she used her magic to send a strong shockwave, which stunned all the attackers on her side of the balcony. They all crumbled to the stone walkway. She turned her head to see a Prowler snarling at her. With a swipe the dagger sliced her face, she too fell instantly to the ground and the Prowler stabbed her in the back. She too was dead. Ana turned to attack the bloodthirsty Prowler with a killing curse but it leapt out of the way, off the balcony and disappeared out of sight. Several killing curses hit the man behind her and he fell over dead. The Akolt members behind her all pointed their wands at her and all at once cast killing curses, some missing and some making contact. Ana fell beside the body of the other woman, the life left her eyes as she laid in a pool of blood. Her eyes staring at the stars in the night sky and her body became still. The Akolt flowed through the halls of the temple, breaking glass, turning over tables and killing anyone in their way.

Outside the temple it was no different; bodies of White Witches were falling one by one at that point. Those who were spared by keeping a distance, fled. A younger Zan was among the fleeing crowd helping carry the wounded away. He and another White Witch stayed behind to hold off the following Akolt members. A killing curse hit the White Witch, but he took down one Akolt member before he too fell to the ground dead. As

Zan turned to flee, a stunning spell hit him and knocked him to the ground.

"Leave the rest!" a voice shouted. "Don't forget why we came here, head back to the temple!" The young Zan looked into the face of his attacker and it was Jeremy.

Jeremy looked down at the young Zan and shook his head with a smirk.

"I told you it would come to this. I'll be the one walking away stronger than ever; you and Ana had your chance. Don't worry; I'm not going to kill you. My master still has hopes for you." He crouched down over Zan.

"You will join us. Not today, not tomorrow, but soon." he said. Zan had tears of fury in his eyes as the young Jeremy stood back up. At the same time the spell wore off, Zan tried to stand, but Jeremy kicked him in the head and he fell back to the ground, unconscious. Jeremy turned his back on Zan's unconscious body and headed back to the temple. Kyle and Dan stood in shock; they couldn't believe what they had just witnessed. The entire time the bloody battles to the death were growing, the more they wanted to help, but they remembered what Mr. Wallis said about the memories.

"They might as well be ghosts' shadows in the night." The image grew blurry and then faded out of sight. They were now back in Mr. and Mrs. Wallis' house again in the very same room. Even though in the memories they were moving, in reality they hadn't budged. The rain still hadn't diminished yet. Silence came over the group as Zan stood and looked at the shocked eyes before him.

"Now you know why I'm giving you the option of leaving." he said with a saddened expression. "That night is one of many I won't ever forget as long as I live. The reason the Akolt attacked was that they thought the Crystal was hidden there. But it wasn't, they were given false information. Their plan had been to take the Crystal and kill all that stood in their way."

Kyle cracked his knuckles with fury and Dan was shaking, but angry too. "Damn those Akolt!" Kyle shouted, his temper rising. "Why? All those spell casters and those innocent people; they didn't stand a chance against those numbers! And to cloud a friend's mind with darkness and hate, it's just wrong."

Dan slammed his fist against the wall in frustration. The two calmed down and Dan stared at Zan. "We're still going with you Zan, you can count on it. We must as they still have May and Christine."

CHAPTER 12

Jeremy's Hideout

In the woods the Prowlers were following Mizori, Thomas and Raphael towards an old house with the back portion of the roof torn off. The windows were missing some glass and the ones not missing were cracked. The colors and design of the house had rotted out through time. Leafy vines had grown from the ground up, nearly covering the whole house. Mizori stepped towards the door on the porch; the porch creaked noisily as she approached the door. She knocked twice. It opened and Mizori ushered in May and Christine as they all went inside. The inside of the house was no different from the outside; the curtains were torn and cobwebs were in every corner. There was a staircase in the center of the entry hall. Mizori grabbed two chairs from the dining room and placed them beside Thomas and Raphael. The two sat May and Christine down in them while Mizori called for Jeremy who was upstairs.

"Jeremy, we have returned with some company."

They heard a door upstairs open with a creak and footsteps moving towards them. At the top of the staircase stood a man wearing a cloak with the hood down, black boots and gloves. He came down the stairs and glanced at May and Christine then looked at Mizori and her group.

"Mizori, I see you and your group came back with these two, but what of the fragment." Mizori handed Jeremy the fragment she had taken from May. "Our Master will be pleased to know that you all remain loyal to him." he said as he took off his gloves and held it up close, his hazel eyes staring back at him through the fragment, as if looking into a mirror.

May wondered how they were going to get out of this situation. Jeremy crouched down beside her.

"I bet you would love to leave," he said looking directly at her.

"Leave her alone," Christine said. Jeremy stood up and went over to her.

"You are of very little interest to us, so if I were you, I would remain silent. Take these two upstairs and put them in the room on the left side of the hallway."

Raphael and Thomas stood the girls up and escorted them upstairs to a dark room and closed the door. Two Prowlers were assigned to guard the hallway. Back in the town, outside of the woods, Kyle, Dan and Zan were preparing to go get May and Christine back. Zan made sure one more time that Kyle and Dan did not want to go back to the Academy.

"Like I'm going back to the Academy and miss out on all the fun" Kyle laughed,

This was the answer Zan expected. The rain had stopped, once again Mr. and Mrs. Wallis wished them the best of luck and said that they would get busy gathering the White Witches and make sure they all knew about the current events. As before, Zan made himself, Kyle and Dan into fog and instantly they were gone. The three of them were back in the woods and both Kyle and Dan experienced the same sickened feeling but not quite as bad as before.

Once the two pulled themselves together, Zan, Kyle and Dan searched for over an hour around the woods.

Zan was confused. "I don't get it," he said still searching. "I teleported us to where I believed the house should be visible."

Dan folded his arms across his chest and began thinking. He remembered how Zan's piece of the Crystal had led them to the other fragments back in the cave when they got close. He saw Zan five feet ahead of him.

"Hey Zan, did you bring your piece of the Crystal?" he asked.

Zan nodded; Kyle was a few feet further ahead of them. Zan gave Dan his container with the crescent fragment sealed inside and it started to glow. The night made it give off a strong visible beam of light, which pointed towards the left. Dan called Kyle over and they started to run towards wherever the beam of light was taking them further into mountains domain. After what seemed like forever, the beam disappeared and the fragment began to glow. They knew they were close. Kyle stopped running and pointed. There it was, the old house was in view. Zan called them over to lay out a plan.

"We all know how this night's going to be and what to expect, so who do we each want to take on?" Dan and Kyle began to think.

134

"I'll take on Raphael" said Kyle.

"That leaves three," said Dan. "I'll take on Thomas, and I'm sure May will take Mizori on if they see each other."

Zan nodded in agreement. The only thing left was to protect Christine. He put the container back in his spell book and they made their way to the old house.

Inside Jeremy was sitting in one of the chairs in the dining room and the fragment he held in his hand was glowing. On the other side of the large table sat Mizori, Raphael and Thomas.

Jeremy stood up and smiled. "They're here. Why don't we go and greet them."

CHAPTER 13

❧

The Battle where it all began

Staying close to each other, Zan, Kyle and Dan made their way to the old house. The door opened as they were approaching the porch. Jeremy stepped outside followed, by Mizori, Raphael and Thomas.

Seeing Zan, Jeremy smiled again. "It's been a while hasn't it Zan?" Kyle took one step closer.

"Where are May and Christine?" he asked. Mizori smiled. Dan knew that any one of the four could attack them at any time and if they didn't, the Prowlers would. Jeremy exchanged looks with the three beside him and then looked back at Zan.

"You and I both know there's only one way you'll get to them, and that is to go through us first." He then pulled out his spell book and wand; Mizori and her group did the same. Dan saw a Prowler approaching from behind. (Jeremy noticed that Dan saw the Prowler and sighed.)

"Mizori, Raphael, Thomas have your fun." In a blink of an eye, Thomas and Raphael pointed their wands at Kyle and Dan, shouted "Limpera!" and both Kyle and Dan were thrown off their feet backwards into the seemingly never ending woods. Raphael and Thomas went after them, leaving Zan who was already fighting with Mizori. Jeremy watched the two duels, clearly amused.

Deep in the woods sparks were flying everywhere as Raphael and Thomas were casting red orbs at Kyle and Dan who were countering with green beams which vanished when they made contact. Back inside the old house Christine and May heard the loud noises and realized a fight had just started. The girls cracked the door slightly to get look into the hallway where they saw a Prowler at the top of the stairs.

The battle continued outside as Mizori shot a bolt of red lightning at Zan who dodged it and then countered with a disarming spell. Mizori's wand flew out of her hand then with a swipe of his wand, Zan sent Mizori soaring into the roof of the house. She then rolled down the crumbling roof and onto the ground. Jeremy cast a red colored spell at Zan who dodged it. Jeremy pointed his wand at precisely the right moment and shouted, sending Zan into the woods near the spot where Kyle and Dan landed. Mizori regained her footing after a hard landing on the ground, shook her dirty hair and ran to grab her wand and spell book that had been knocked out of her hands. Knowing that Jeremy was fighting Zan, she ran inside to make sure the Prowlers were doing their job of guarding the girls. As she approached the staircase she saw May trying to sneak past the Prowler guarding the top of the stairs. Mizori pointed her wand and cast a red orb.

When the Prowler saw Mizori pointing her wand, it turned to see May and made to grab her not realizing it had stepped into the path of the orb. The blue ball hit the Prowler's side, sending it slamming into the wall, creating a large hole. The Prowler vanished into woods. May and Christine made a run for it to the other side of the hallway as more spells flew past them, leaving burnt circles on the wall. Mizori continued down the long hallway to find where the girls where hiding.

Back outside flames hit the ground beside Kyle who had just cast another green beam at Raphael. Making a single swipe with his wand, Raphael sent the jinx back at Kyle, hitting him in the shoulder. "Give it up kid." he said, not amused by his opponent's spell casting. Kyle was knocked to his knees and reached to grab his shoulder, which had just been hit by his own hex. Raphael put his wand back in his cloak pocket and stretched out his free hand. He cast a small jolt of red lightning that hit Kyle in the chest and knocked him to the ground.

"I don't even have to use my wand to kill you. Face it, you're out-classed!" Kyle saw Raphael's face and saw that even he was at his limit for spell casting. This meant that Dan and Thomas would also be reaching their limit. At that moment Kyle had an idea, if he could just reach Dan in time they may be able to win. Kyle rose with a chuckle.

"Sorry to break it to you but I don't give up that easily." With just enough energy left, he shot a paralyzing spell at Raphael, who dodged it. Kyle ran to where he saw flickers of red and yellow lights followed by sparks. Thomas dodged a disarming spell, turned, and with a swipe of his wand sent

Dan twisting backwards onto the ground. Thomas then put his wand back in his cloak pocket and walked towards Dan.

"I believe it's time to end this little fight," he said as he opened his free hand. Red and black threads were shooting out of his palm and his spell book began to glow dark blue. Dan quickly got up and started to run towards Kyle's calls in the distance. They were a couple feet away now and Raphael was doing the same thing as Thomas with his now open palm turned back. Both Raphael and Thomas stretched out there arms and aimed them at their running targets. As Kyle neared Dan, he shouted.

"Dan, when I say go we slide!" Both of their attackers were too busy focusing on their own spells. Kyle and Dan were about four feet apart and their timing could not have been any better.

"Now Dan, slide!" As they slid on the ground, both spells were already shot. Kyle's plan worked perfectly and as he lifted his head he saw that both Thomas and Raphael's spells hit the other caster and both of them were sent twirling twenty feet backwards. When the two hit the ground they were both conscious but couldn't move as they had used up their energy for the last spell.

"This isn't over. We'll meet again soon and next time neither of you will be any luckier than your father, Dan." Raphael said to Kyle and Dan as they were running away, back to the old house.

Dan stopped for a moment and turned to look at Raphael. "I'd love to see you try to make good on that threat," he said with a glare and turned his back, and continued walking. Kyle followed leaving Thomas and Raphael where they laid, struggling to get up without success.

"Hey Dan, I'm sorry. I didn't know," said Kyle who had now caught up with Dan. Dan just kept walking, doing his best to avoid making eye contact.

"It's alright," he said as he looked up at the night sky.

CHAPTER 14

&

Learning a New Way of Spell Casting

Kyle remembered that Dan still had May's spell book. If May was to have a fighting chance, they would have to hurry and get to her and Christine before a Prowler or Mizori did. Back inside the old house, May and Christine were hiding in a room on the right side of the hallway close to the staircase. With a loud 'Crack!' Mizori blasted all the doors open one by one with magic, intending to scare her targets out of hiding. She began checking each room as she made her way down the hallway. As she drew closer, May slowly made her way to the now opened door as Mizori checked one of the empty rooms. The girls were looking for an opportunity to escape.

"OK Christine, we need to move fast before she finds us," she whispered, cautiously crawling out of the room and making her way to the staircase. Success! Christine made her way to the opened door following May's path. She heard Mizori's footsteps coming back into the hall and preparing to check the next room. "Come out little ones and I promise I'll make it quick," she said as she went inside the opened doorway.

It was now or never. Taking a deep breath, Christine crawled out of the only room left for inspection. May peeked out over the top of the steps where she was crouching and waved for Christine to hurry. She made it just as Mizori stepped out of the previous room and prepared to enter the last room in the hallway, the room where the girls had been hiding. As May and Christine were beginning their quiet descent down the stairs, Christine placed a foot on a stair that gave a creaking sound. Mizori stepped out of their previous hiding spot and walked over to the staircase with her wand pointing straight ahead. The two girls ran out of the front door and across the front porch just as a Prowler who leaped from the roof of the house and landed a few feet from them stopping them in their tracks.

Another Prowler dropped out of the trees to join the one that had dropped from the roof-top. May and Christine had nowhere to go; if they tried running Mizori would surely stop them with another spell, and the Prowlers had them blocked. Christine gave May a questioning look.

"Can't you just use one of your spells?" May shook her head no.

"I can only do that if I have my spell book." Mizori came out of the old house and made her way to where the girls were standing.

"So this is where I find you," she said with a wicked grin. "Tell me dear, would you like to see your mom and sister again? Do you recognize my voice now little one? That's right; I was the cloaked person that afternoon."

May's eyes widened in shock; before her she saw a flash of her mother telling her to run and a loud bang at the door as someone was trying to blast open the locked door. "It wasn't easy, but in the end even she couldn't stop me. With her decision to stay behind to help your sister instead of escaping with you and your father, I simply put them both out of their misery."

Another flashback as May was remembering her house being burnt to the ground and her dad pulling her away from the inferno. Coming back to earth May was looking at Mizori who was just about to use a levitation spell on her and Christine when Kyle and Dan came rushing to their aid. With his last bit of waning energy, Dan's last three spells were cast. He hit the two Prowlers, sending them soaring into the night's darkness, while Mizori deflected the other. Kyle quickly tossed May her spell book and stepped in front of Christine, telling her to stay close. May had sheer determination in her eyes and with perfect timing cast two disarming spells. Mizori dodged the first and then a levitation spell hit Mizori as she was preparing to counter with her own spell. May lifted her up and sent her flipping into the woods behind them. Kyle and Dan nodded at May and wondered where she had learned how to use that spell in such a short time. Now safe again for the moment, Christine quickly looked into the woods.

"Where's Zan?" she asked.

"Oh yea, he must still be fighting Jeremy," Dan said as he ran towards the sound of sparks. The other three followed behind.

Zan was at his limit, as was Jeremy, who had just taken another one of Zan's spell in the chest.

"Enough! It's time to end this!" he spat as he put his wand back in his cloak pocket. Zan did the same and then both of their spell books began to glow. Both Jeremy and Zan opened their free hands; Jeremy's hand was shooting out the same dark blue threads as Thomas and Raphael's had earlier while Zan's palm was shooting out light blue threads. Even the fragments of the Crystal started to glow; both were ready to give it their all with their last spell. They looked at each other.

"This is for our friends and, more importantly, this is for me. This time I'll be the one walking away!" Zan shouted, and they started circling each other. With every circle made, the farther apart they went. Then they rushed at each other, pulling their open palms back.

"You still haven't learned, have you?!" Jeremy yelled as he fired his spell at Zan who quickly dodged it. The spell slid across the ground and vanished.

"Actually, I learned plenty," Zan said as he shot back at Jeremy. The shot went right through Jeremy's spell book that he was using as a shield and then hit him in the chest with such force that when the spell vanished, Jeremy had steam all around him. He fell to his knees in shock, and dropped his spell book and it landed face down. He looked back at Zan impressed and he too collapsed. As he fell, the fragment of the Crystal fell out of Jeremy's sleeve and bounced several feet away and the glowing stopped. He laid motionless, but still managed to laugh as blood from his mouth ran down his cheek.

"Well done. I'm impressed Zan. You still have it in you, but don't think you've won. I'm not finished with you yet."

Jeremy's body began to turn to ash. His body became a torn window curtain. Zan crouched down to remove the fabric to see a wooden stick figure that had been split in half. Zan picked up the top half.

"Well I'll be damned. You actually managed to master a spell this strong have you?" he thought to himself. Kyle, Dan, May and Christine found Zan and rushed to his side.

"Well, it looks like we are too late to assist Jeremy now. So he decided to leave without us," said Mizori, hiding behind a tree eying Zan's group. She had a cut on her face and her right arm was tied to her chest with a piece of torn cloak, forming a homemade sling which gave the clear impression that her arm was broken. Thomas and Raphael were both clutching their chests; Raphael limped over for a peek.

"I hate to be called a coward as much as you, but sometimes in these situations you need to take what you can and leave." he said to her as they began to rush towards the fragment. Zan told Kyle to go get the fragment that fell out of Jeremy's sleeve. As he bent to pick it up, a jet of purple came from behind the trees and knocked him aside; Mizori rushed towards the fragment, followed by Thomas and Raphael, who were still clutching their chests.

"I believe this is ours, boy," she said to Kyle in a threatening tone as she picked up the fragment with her left hand, backing up to Thomas and Raphael. With more than enough energy for spell casting, she turned herself, Raphael and Thomas into navy blue fog clouds and together they soared away over the trees and into the night.

Zan and his group went back towards the old house; the girls stayed very close together. The boys could tell that they were becoming very good friends. Zan and the boys were beyond exhausted, and as they drifted into a deep coma-like sleep, the last thing they heard were the quiet voices of the girls. The morning had come and the sun was just rising over the mountains. In the growing light, everyone could see how badly damaged they were. Kyle and Dan's shirts were torn and had dried blood that had run down their lips. Zan's shirt and cloak was torn from the front and back but his jeans had only minor tears and he had a bloody nose. May and Christine had a few cuts and bruises on their arms and legs but were in otherwise in good shape. May was looking down at the ground.

"Hey, what's wrong?" asked Dan. May looked up.

"It's nothing, forget it," she said. On cobweb infested couch, Zan was finally waking up.

"So how did you defeat Mizori and the other two?" he asked them curiously. Kyle started to grin with confidence.

"I saw how easily Raphael could underestimate his opponents, so I made him chase after me.

When I came to where Dan was fighting Thomas, we had planned to use their spells against them, and it worked. As for Mizori, May gave her a free flying lesson."

Zan nodded in amazement that they were able to beat them. However he knew as well as they did that what had happened this time wouldn't work again. Zan gathered everyone together and they began the long walk back.

"Zan what is that?" asked Kyle noticing the top half of the stick figure Zan was examining.

"You mean this? Well, this is a substitution item. Very advanced dark magic, you put your own blood on an inanimate object that you want to represent yourself."

"Really?" asked Kyle gulping at the sound of using blood for magic.

"Oh, yes. Like I said, it's dark magic. And from the looks of what Jeremy used in this substitution, it was to make a copy of himself."

"A copy?!?" said May joining in, suddenly with great interest.

"Yes, a copy," said Zan, coolly. "However, the copy itself is but a cheap imitation and like a puppet master, Jeremy would have to control his puppet from afar,"

Late in the day, as the group was only about an hour away from reaching Willow's Den, May finally approached Zan and asked permission for Christine to join the group.

"No," said Zan, sensing the curiosity of those around him. As they continued to walk May told him that her aunt knew Christine's great uncle and that he had been married to a White Witch. Christine had never known that her great uncle was married to a member of their clan because he died when Christine was a baby. May continued trying to convince Zan to let her friend continue with them.

"I know she's a mortal but she's really smart and you have to admit she's been a huge help."

Zan looked down at her and said, "May, we promised her brother Ren that we would find her and bring her home. On top of that what would the rest of the Witches think of a mortal being involved with our problems?"

"Well, Zan, she did have or has relatives that are White Witches so that should count for something, and she thinks that the Wallis' know her parents," May grew silent to allow Zan some time to think as they made their way into Willow's Den.

As the group drew closer to their destination, Christine eased alongside Kyle and said.

"Thanks for protecting me back there," Kyle looked at Christine then turned his head.

"No problem," he said now looking straight ahead. "Besides a mortal like you would've easily been killed if I hadn't. Hey, why don't you take your winter hat off? You must be having a heat-stroke," Christine then took her eyes off Kyle and also looked ahead.

"Thanks, but I prefer to keep it on. I've grown used to wearing it a lot lately," Finally, after walking all day from the old broken down house, Zan and the others reached Willow's Den. The townspeople looked at Zan and his group as they came out of the woods in shock and curiosity.

"What the heck happened to them?" asked a man at a nearby shop.

"Don't know, but must have been one helluva' night," said another.

As Zan and the kids walked past the crowds of curious and scared onlookers, Zan spotted Mr. Wallis at a grocery store and called over to him. Mr. Wallis, like the other people in the area, was shocked at their appearance. He rushed over to escort them to his house, where his wife quickly opened the door and let them all in. Mr. Wallis reassured the curious onlookers and sent them on their way. Kyle, Dan, Zan, May, and Christine were all just glad to be away from the eyes of the scores of townspeople outside. They all sat in the living room. The kids sat on the couch while Mr. and Mrs. Wallis sat in pulled up chairs along with Zan.

"What the devil happened out there?" asked Mr. Wallis anxiously.

"We ran in to Jeremy and the three stooges in that accursed place," replied Zan. "Jeremy's gone. Escaped. And Mizori took the fragment of the Crystal and fled with Raphael and Thomas."

Mrs. Wallis looked even more curious as she looked at Kyle and the others sitting on the couch.

"Then you kids took on Mizori and her group on your own while Zan battled Jeremy?" she asked.

"Yep, but those guys know there spells really well," said Dan.

"I'll get all of you some water and wet towels," said Mrs. Wallis as her husband fixed his gaze upon the four kids, obviously quite impressed.

"Hey, Zan? Why didn't you just teleport all of us here as you did when we went to save May and Christine?" asked Dan. Zan coughed and looked away.

"It must have slipped my mind," he replied, not wanting to see Kyle and Dan's expressions of disbelief. When Mrs. Wallis got back from the kitchen with water and towels, Kyle, May and Dan knew they had to ask Zan sooner or later to teach them. So Kyle got Zan's attention as he was cleaning his wounds. As he blotted the wet towel on his cuts and rinsed it in the bowl Mrs. Wallis had brought, the water turned to pink.

"Zan, we were wondering if you could teach us how to spell cast with a wand too?" asked Kyle tentatively. He now had Zan thinking.

"Not me, kid. Forget it. But I bet some of the White Witches would teach you guys. In fact there are some in Guardian's Peak. If anyone could teach you three at the moment it would be them. However, in the end it's your choice to spell cast with a wand or not," said Zan as he cleaned his wounds. The pink water dribbled down his skin and into his socks.

"Yea? When will that be?" asked Kyle disappointed by Zan's answer.

"Patience kid; you three will learn but not as soon as you would like to. We still have to search for possible fragments in this area."

It was a blow to the three spell casters in training, but they expected such an answer from Zan. Christine asked Mr. and Mrs. Wallis if she could use a phone to call her parents in Guardian's Peak. The two nodded with obvious pleasure and Mr. Wallis showed her where the phone was. Kyle and the others hadn't had time to get a good look at the inside of the house when they had walked in earlier. The living room was decorated with paintings of the most remarkable hills and ocean views they have ever seen. The curtains on the windows were a bright blue just like the ocean and the whole house had a calmness about it that made everyone feel at ease.

Once Christine had finished her phone call, she returned to the living room and sat back on her side of the couch.

"Zan, I talked to my parents and they were at first very concerned. But when I told them I was with the Wallis' and that I had made new friends that I would like hang out with a little more, they reluctantly reconsidered and told me to call every day and were very happy that I was safe. And besides, I haven't had this much excitement happen in a long, long time."

Mr. and Mrs. Wallis told Zan and his group that they could stay with them for as long as they liked and until they figured out where they would be going next. After they thanked the couple for all their kind hospitality, they went up the stairs to the guest rooms and took turns in the shower and changed into clean clothes.

"Seriously, teleportation would've been faster; why didn't you do it?" asked Kyle.

"I told you already it must have slipped my mind!" Zan hissed.

"Don't give me that crap! You made us walk all the way here for your own pleasure!" protested Kyle standing up and pointing a finger at Zan who raised a free hand to cast a silencing spell on Kyle.

Kyle tried to roar out in outrage to make Zan release his spell on him but only lip syncing could be seen.

"Hmm.... quite an improvement, Kyle. I could get used to it," said Dan with his arms folded.

CHAPTER 15

It has only just begun

Somewhere in a neighborhood of Guardian's Peak a group of hooded figures headed towards a house that had its lights dimmed. One of them knocked on the door and the voices from inside the house stopped; the door opened and another figure with a hood greeted them.

"Oh, it's you three. Come on in. We were expecting you." he said as the three walked in. Once inside, and the door closed, they saw a whole group of hooded figures that were sitting at the dining room table. All eyes were on the three that had just walked in.

"Come, sit, we need to talk about the problem. Mizori, get your arm fixed. As for you two, you're lucky that your injuries aren't serious," said one of the figures sitting across the table, noticing the holes in both Raphael and Thomas's cloaks and Mizori's broken arm. There were perhaps a dozen of them there. Mizori went up to one of the hooded figures and a hand which glowed a bright yellow emerged from the cloak and took her arm. Only seconds later the hand withdrew and Mizori took her healed right arm out of her homemade sling and got rid of it. She stretched her now perfectly healed arm as she grabbed a chair and sat at the table. Thomas and Raphael also grabbed chairs and joined the group. Now everyone waited for the figure at the end of the table to speak. They all knew why they were there.

"I thought the White Witches no longer posed a threat to us," said a woman's voice at the table. They all nodded in agreement.

"Yes, and only a handful remain. The rest have either gone their separate ways or died out through the years. Just like us, they're short on followers and will be searching for new ones," said another woman.

The figure sitting at the head of the table stretched out his left hand towards Mizori. It was clear that he wanted the fragment. Mizori slid the fragment across the table to him. He picked it up, examined it closely and grinned broadly at it.

"I see your mission was a success. Where's Jeremy?" he asked. Raphael looked at him.

"Marco, he's preparing for another match with Zan," said Raphael. The rest of the figures started to talk among themselves.

"I see, No matter. What's important now is that we find new followers," he said, giving the fragment to the short plump hooded man sitting beside him and telling him to give it to their Master later on. Everyone started to consider who would be good allies. Marco, sitting at the end of the table, thought for a few seconds and it finally came to him.

"I know exactly who we need. I think they will prove to be useful. Knowing the White Witches, they will be thinking the same thing," he said as once again all turned to listen to Marco.

"Mizori, Raphael, Thomas. You have a new assignment. I want you to go find a large group for me. I believe you already know which group I'm talking about. You already know a couple of them," he said as he slid two cards that had pictures on them over to the trio. Thomas picked them up and recognized the two.

"Ah, yes. I remember those two," he said, passing the cards to Raphael who looked at them and nodded in agreement. Marco stood up.

"No need for you three or any of us to worry about Zan's group. They will still be out of their league even if they do start to learn new ways to spell cast. As for the rest of you, our other followers have discovered where many of the remaining fragments can be found. Now go, go to Southeast Asia, the Dutch Caribbean and the Virgin Islands, to the Horn of Africa and find them."

The meeting was done and one by one left the house, leaving Marco with Mizori, Raphael and Thomas. They turned to look at the man in front of them as his light green eyes gazed at them.

"You three know your assignment. Get going and find those mutts,"

Mizori and her group left, closing the door and leaving Marco inside the house alone.

At about the same time, Zan and his group received word to go to certain areas where there might be more fragments of the Crystal and to recover more of the the fragments lost. He also told Mr. and Mrs. Wallis that Christine knew what they were and reassured them that she was to be more than trustworthy enough for keeping their secrets. Christine would spend time with Mr. and Mrs. Wallis or with her older brother at his shop in Luna's Berg, partly to help him with the business and partly to spend time with him. While Christine was helping her brother in the hardware store, she stayed in the upstairs room above the store, and caught up with schoolwork. She and Ren had always been homeschooled so it was a familiar task.

The next few weeks were busy; Zan and his group took many trips and were successful in finding most of the fragments. The month of December was colder than usual; the Academy in Misty Road now had all students and faculty wearing jackets, jeans, and other clothing inside as well as outdoors for warmth. Inside the spell casting rooms for newcomers, they were learning about the four elements and how to use simple magic to cast spells for changing the colors of leaves and making closed objects open at will. In the higher grades, the trainees next year would become magicians and in their eighth year, if they were lucky, they would become spell casters, and perhaps someday be given the opportunity to become new members of the White Witches. The Mistress sat at the table accompanied by two members of the White Witches who were standing on opposite sides of the office door.

"Mistress, the time for gathering new allies is drawing nearer. No doubt the Akolt knows this too," said the woman standing to the left of the door. The other woman also standing at the door nodded in agreement. The Mistress closed her eyes for a few moments, deep in thought, and then opened them with a very serious look on her face.

"Alright, very well, who did you have in mind Cassidy?" Cassidy looked at her companion then back at the Mistress and sighed.

"The Clan," she said in a shy manner. The other woman looked at Cassidy.

"We can't, they're neutral and they don't want any part in our problems," Cassidy had her head down, embarrassed for coming up with the idea.

"Ss... Sorry Fiona, it was just a thought," she said looking down at her shoes.

The Mistress thought for another moment and then smiled at them "No Cassidy, don't be. We're going to need all the ideas you and the rest of the White Witches have to offer," And with that said, the two women exited the office, leaving the Mistress in deep thought. After sitting in silence for a few minutes she stood up, left her office and started to walk down the hall. She thought to herself as she caught glimpses of students, both magic and non-magic.

"That's right, if we're going to defeat the Akolt and bring an end to this nightmare, I'm afraid all possible assistance is necessary this time. I only hope that we're all prepared for what is to come."

She continued to stroll through the halls and then went outside where the freezing air greeted her. She continued to think to herself

"Zan, you better take great care of the students accompanying you... and yourself." On the field Collin, Will and William were practicing their spell casting.

"Not bad, but let's see you deflect this next one!" shouted Collin. He had shot a stunning spell at William; once again it was rendered useless because he had surrounded himself with a magical shield. Will broke William's magical shield and hoisted him up with a levitation spell.

"Whoa! Okay, you got me, now put me down," William roared, and Will put him down gently.

"Nice round of practice guys," said Collin. They soon spotted their group leader headed toward them.

"Well, I see you're all practicing hard on your spells and doing very well. Come along now, the Mistress wants to have a brief talk with all the magic students."

Inside the meeting room the Mistress stood at her desk looking down at the faces of each and every spell caster there.

"Alright now listen up. Starting after the summer break, those who are sixteen and up will have the chance to sign up and be placed in a series of three test provided by the Academy and monitored by high ranking members of The White Witches. Between now and then all of you will continue for the rest of the school year learning your spells. It's imperative that you are able to master the skills. Keep in mind as I speak to you now, this is important, as the forces of darkness are planning on getting their hands on this and any others they can find."

She held up a fragment and made sure everyone could see it. The Counselors and White Witches in the room stared at it, their eyes widening.

"I thought Zan was the only one who had one." said Cassidy, quite surprised.

"This fragment is one of many and they all belong to none other than the Crystal of Light."

Complete silence shadowed the room. "Ah, damn. That means were gonna' have to fight, aren't we?" Will said, breaking the silence.

The Mistress' light green eyes stared at him. "Yes Will, if push comes to shove then we will have to fight. And that's why all of you will be learning all the new spells from the Elites. We will start after summer; all exams will be canceled. So I wish the best of luck to each and every one of you. The Akolt are growing stronger and we'll need all the support we can get. That is all. Now, off to your regular routines."

Leaving the meeting room the trainees were scared and nervous about what the future held. William called over to Kate.

"Did you hear? Jeez before we know it we'll all be up to our necks in countless battles."

"Better late than never." said Collin, cutting in on the conversation. "Can't wait to show those Akolt members how we trainees do things around here."

"You're full of it." Kate snapped. "This is serious. If the Akolt get their hands on the fragments of the Crystal and repair it... Don't look at me like that. You know the story!" The two boys nodded in agreement. The rest of the day everyone was constantly talking about what was to come and when that time did come, what they had to do to be ready.

CHAPTER 16

❧

Winter Party and Crow's Warning

On Christmas Eve, Christine and Ren came over to spend the night at Mr. and Mrs. Wallis' house. After spending time with the Wallis', the two had become really close with the older couple. It was cold outside and the ghastly winds of autumn seemed to have finally come to a halt. No more threatening dark clouds lay overhead. The cloudless night was blanketed with stars across the entire the sky which illuminated the night with a rare beauty. The moon was in its crescent form.

"You know traveling with these people is a mistake," said Ren to his sister who rolled her eyes and sighed.

"Not you too Ren, just because I told you and the others…"

"I'm only telling you what Crow told me." Ren interrupted calmly.

"Crow told you that, did he? It figures, leave it to Crow to find the worst in everyone we meet. Only he would make such a comment like that."

"Yes, but don't forget he's right most of the time. And he won't like seeing all of them in the mountains of Guardian's Peak." he said as his sister knocked on the Wallis' door. As they entered they all greeted each other in delight. Even Zan managed to smile at the two.

The house was filled with the delicious aroma of Christmas Eve dinner. Kyle, Dan, and May got regular letters from their parents and the Academy wishing them a Happy Christmas and they all took an unusual delight in writing back. At dinnertime Mr. Wallis served his famous ham and his wife's sweet potatoes. While the large group gathered around the table and began to devour the food around them, Zan had the good news the group needed to hear. He began to tell them the news after emptying his glass of wine.

"I just got a call today from our friends in the Academy in Misty Road. We are almost in the clear, they have started to consider allowing Christine to accompany us on our search for the fragments. The Head Mistress will let us know her decision by next week."

"Also, the next fragment is said to be in Guardian's Peak, so we will be traveling there soon. While we're there Christine can visit her parents and there will be people there to help you three with what you have to learn. And if that is not enough, Mr. Wallis told me Master Michael has finished his Assignment and will also be there." Kyle, Dan and May were delighted to know that what Zan meant is that they would finally learn a new way of spell casting. They also had questions for Master Michael, for only he would know the answers. Christine looked at across the table at Kyle's face as they all stood up to put the dishes away. May noticed and walked over.

"So, Christine? Taken a liking to Kyle, have you?" she said smiling. "You know, despite his foolish actions, one grows used to him."

Christine looked at May and wondered what foolish actions she was referring to. May smiled at her. "You'll see what I mean," She then walked over to Dan, who was sitting on the couch reading.

"I really wonder if these kids have what it takes to become the next generation of White Witches someday?" Zan thought to himself as he and Mr. and Mrs. Wallis finished putting the remaining dishes away. Kyle was carrying on a conversation with Ren.

Christine looked out the window and saw snow falling outside, its white flakes hitting the ground and covering shops and houses. She walked closer to the window and stared outside.

"Oh, it's so pretty," she said as Dan, Kyle and Christine gathered at the other windows to gaze at the white flakes as they fell from the night sky. At that moment, Zan knew that when Kyle, Dan, and May's school semester was over, new challenges were in store and their hunt for the remaining fragments of the Crystal would continue.

Epilogue

In this world, there are many Crystals of Light - from the museums to the caves of great mystery and wonder. Each Crystal making beautiful even the darkest places, but there's one that has been kept away from all eyes until now...

Mortals like you and me aren't the only ones on this planet. For there are others who have extraordinary abilities; Kyle Fang is one of these people whose life, along with the rest of his kind, would change when he and his friends will become a part of a war that was once at an end, but will begin again.

Acknowledgements

The single hardest part of writing the Darkness of Light series is making sure that I thank the countless people who have helped me and taken an interest therefore I must begin with an apology to anyone I may have forgotten and I trust you will forgive me.

The only place to start is at the beginning which begins with thanking Aunt Jodi for telling me stories when I was little and, of course, my teachers Verian Aguilar, Thames Shaw, Leslie Penther, Karen Oscar, Mary Howe, Rebecca McDonnell, Margo Lynch, Stephanie Flaherty, Jennifer Rejim, Willie Wilson, Adam Quandt and of course Coach Fred Hupprich. I also owe a special thanks to Dan Kinzer, Brian Hennelly, Barbara Manning, Kenneth O'Bryhim, Stuart Crouch, Dan Cwik, Victor Boulanger and Francis Koolman and the countless others who helped along the way. Of course, all of my friends and

Acknowledgements

classmates from Antilles School in St. Thomas, Virgin Islands and at the International School of Curaçao in Emmastad, Curaçao in the Dutch Caribbean.

I was inspired by the Summer Academic Adventure Program at Asheville School and am thankful for the time spent at Paw-Paw's farm, Davey's Branch, which borders the Pisgah National Forest in Mill's River in Western North Carolina, which provided a backdrop for many of the settings herein.

It is with pleasure that I thank my Mom and Dad and my sister, Jordan, for their endless encouragement, confidence and support and for putting up with me and this novel even though it often overlapped with school. When things bogged down, I could always think of the humor of my uncles, Hap Ray, J.P. McBryde and Jordan Lea and the patience of my aunts Susan Ray, Cathy Lea and Karen Lea McBryde (who will be publishing her long-awaited novels very soon). I hope my cousin Niki Medlin, her husband Ronnie and their kids Kaeli and Blake, and my cousin Jenni Ray and her children Cassidy and Mason, and cousins Mary Katherine Ray, Lea, Roston and Gillie McBryde, and Thomas Lea all enjoy this book.

I would also like to thank my godparents Thorpe and Francie McKenzie for always remembering me and a special mention for Buffett and Bruiser who always stayed close by my writing chair. Lastly, I owe a special thanks to Gordon S. Black for his support, advice and encouragement. And again, know that if I forgot to mention you, please know your support was truly appreciated nonetheless. And last but certainly not least, many thanks to all of you who enjoyed the book and are looking forward to the next in the Darkness of Light series.

About the Author

The author, Hap Lea, was born in Paraguay as Ismael Godoy in 1992 and has had the privilege of traveling widely including visits to parts of Africa and Europe as well as North and South America. After moving to the United States as a toddler, he subsequently attended grade school in St. Thomas in the U.S. Virgin Islands and a graduate of the International School of Curaçao in the Dutch Antilles where he has lived for the past three years.

He looks forward to extended visits to China, Japan, and Taiwan, an overland journey to South America and to departing the Caribbean for university in the United States. When he is not writing, he enjoys reading fiction, Japanese manga and classic novels and is an avid viewer of educational programs such as those on the Discovery Channel and the History Channel. He is now working on the fourth novel of the *Darkness of Light* series. For more information on the series or to reach Hap, please visit www.hap-lea.com.

CPSIA information can be obtained at www.ICGtesting.com
Printed in the USA
BVOW02s1435100516

447523BV00019B/88/P